"I've wanted to do that for a while," *he murmured as he drew back from* *the kiss.*

"Have you?" she whispered.

"Frankie," he muttered, his fingertips trailing down her throat. "Just so we're clear—this has nothing to do with this game we're playing." His gaze flicked to the base of her throat where his thumb stroked over the fast race of her pulse. "I want you."

His blunt words widened Frankie's eyes and sent heat flooding through her body. "Eli, I don't..." she managed to get out.

He stopped her with a fingertip across her lips. "I'm not saying I want out of our deal to fool Harry. I just want you to know that if I'm kissing you—" he paused, his eyes going hotter "—or anything else physical, I'm not acting."

Dear Reader,

Collaborating with friends Chris Flynn, Pat Kay and Allison Leigh to create our second Hunt for Cinderella miniseries ranks in my top-ten, most-fun-ever projects. We four had so much fun brainstorming these books. Billionaire Harry Hunt has turned his matchmaking focus on the four Fairchild sisters—and in my story, Frankie Fairchild is determined to foil his benevolent scheming. But when she enlists childhood crush Eli Wolf in a plan to stymie Harry, she gets far more than a coconspirator—because Eli is the one man Frankie has never been able to resist. And unknown to Frankie, Eli's more than ready to convince her he's the one man she can trust with her heart.

I hope you enjoy Frankie and Eli's story—and that you'll return next month for *Meet Mr. Prince* by Patricia Kay for the final installment in The Hunt for Cinderella series.

Happy reading!

Lois

BEAUTY AND THE WOLF

LOIS FAYE DYER

Silhouette®

SPECIAL EDITION®

Published by Silhouette Books

America's Publisher of Contemporary Romance

SILHOUETTE BOOKS

Recycling programs
for this product may
not exist in your area.

ISBN-13: 978-0-373-65573-1

BEAUTY AND THE WOLF

Visit Silhouette Books at www.eHarlequin.com

Printed in U.S.A.

Books by Lois Faye Dyer

Silhouette Special Edition

LOIS FAYE DYER

lives in a small town on the shore of beautiful Puget Sound in the Pacific Northwest with her two eccentric and lovable cats, Chloe and Evie. She loves to hear from readers. You can write to her c/o Paperbacks Plus, 1618 Bay Street, Port Orchard, WA 98366. Visit her on the web at www.LoisDyer.com.

For Michael, Stefanie, Randall, Lilia and Ava—
you're the best family possible

Chapter One

The living room of Harry Hunt's lakeside mansion in Seattle glowed with warm light. Two matching Tiffany chandeliers were suspended from the high ceiling at each end of the spacious room, their stained-glass flowers vibrant with color. Outside, the rain and wind of a Pacific Northwest storm picked up speed as it raced across Lake Washington to hammer against the window glass. Inside, the people gathered in the big room were warm and comfortable, thanks to the fire crackling in the hearth beneath the hand-carved cedar mantel.

Frankie Fairchild rose from an overstuffed armchair and crossed the room to the bar, leaving her mother, Cornelia, chatting animatedly with Lily Hunt. Several bottles were clustered on the gleaming mahogany surface, and Frankie chose one with a distinctive label. The tart white wine from the Chateau Ste. Michelle Winery just north of Seattle was a personal favorite. She tilted the bottle to refill her glass.

As she sipped from the stemmed crystal, her gaze drifted idly over the room, pausing at the sight of her cousin Justin's little daughter, Ava, hopping along the edge of the oriental wool carpet.

Harry's neighbor, local actress Madge Edgley, bent to speak to Ava as the child reached the quartet of people chatting together on the bright red and blue carpet.

Harry always invites the nicest mix of friends and interesting people to his get-togethers, Frankie thought with appreciation. She moved on, noting familiar faces in the groups of people scattered around the long room, until she reached the group of men standing in front of the fireplace. Her uncle Harry and his son Justin were deep in conversation with two other men. Frankie knew one of them—Nicholas Dean—only slightly. The fourth man she knew very well. Eli Wolf was tall and broad-shouldered, with black hair and a rugged handsomeness that could make a woman's heart stutter if he smiled directly at her.

Eli looked up, snaring her with an intent look from smoky blue eyes. Frankie froze, unable to look away.

It wasn't until he turned to answer a question from Harry that Frankie realized she'd been holding her breath, caught by that enigmatic, very male stare.

She spun around to face the bar, topping off her wine with faintly trembling fingers.

What on earth is wrong with me?

Ever since Eli had given her a kiss at her last birthday party, she'd been thinking about him much too often. The kiss had sizzled, smoked, even though it was too short. In fact, the memory of his mouth on hers hadn't faded in the four months since; if she closed her eyes, she could still feel the heat. She'd actually conducted an experiment over the last couple of months, purposefully kissing three other very attractive men. Though all three were adept, practiced and assured at kissing, none of them had stirred one iota of serious interest, let alone lust. She'd felt nothing remotely resembling what she'd felt with Eli. Zero. Zip. Nada.

It was very annoying.

She couldn't decide what to do about it, if anything. And inaction was so unlike her that her inability to decisively resolve the issue and put it behind her was worrisome.

"Frankie." A friendly pat on her shoulder accompanied the greeting. "How are you, honey?"

She turned around, glad of the distraction from her thoughts, smiling with affection at the tall, lanky man who was her host. "I'm good, Uncle Harry." She glanced over his shoulder. "I thought you were busy talking business with Nicholas."

"I was." Harry's shrewd gaze went from Frankie's face and down the length of the room to the fireplace, where the owner of Dean Construction stood with Justin and Eli. "I must say I'm impressed with Nicholas. He's built his daddy's construction company into a solid corporation, despite strong competition. I'd bet money he'll triple his net worth in the next five years."

"You're rarely wrong about these things, so he must be an excellent businessman." Frankie sipped her white wine, her gaze following Harry's. There was no question Nicholas Dean's appearance backed up Harry's assessment of his potential for success; he fairly oozed self-confidence. He was tall, well built and had an air of easy, affable friendliness that was belied by his sharply intelligent eyes. His presence here tonight, at a gathering of Harry's family and personal friends, was significant. Frankie met Harry's eyes once again. "You're thinking of giving him the contract for building the new HuntCom campus in south Seattle, aren't you?" she guessed.

"I'm considering it." Harry nodded. "I've narrowed the list down to two—it's between him and Eli."

"Hmm." Frankie wasn't surprised. Elijah Wolf was the head of Wolf Construction and fiercely competitive. He and Justin were in their thirties now and remained close, although Justin was married, with a little girl, and Eli was still a bachelor.

"If Nicholas gets the contract, we'll be seeing a lot more of him," Harry told her.

"Mmm-hmm," Frankie murmured.

"Whoever gets the job will be working closely with my boys, of course," he went on, "but Eli's practically a member of the family already, while Nicholas isn't as well known to us."

"Wouldn't it be easier, then, if you awarded the contract to Eli and his brothers at Wolf Construction?"

Harry shrugged. "Maybe. But if I don't give Dean Construction fair consideration for the job, it smacks of nepotism."

Frankie choked on a sip of wine. Harry immediately clapped a big hand against her back, thumping her between her shoulder blades.

"Are you all right?" he asked with concern.

"I'm fine, Uncle Harry," she got out. She coughed to clear her throat and took another sip of wine. "It was the shock of hearing you mention nepotism as if it were a bad thing," she said, tongue in cheek.

"I don't practice nepotism," he growled defensively.

Frankie laughed, her amusement drawing a reluctant grin from Harry.

"All right," he said with a shrug. "Maybe I tend to take care of my family first, but is that a crime?"

Frankie gave him an impulsive hug, the familiar scent of his aftershave warming her with affectionate memories. "No, Uncle Harry, it's not."

"Well, then…" He wrapped an arm around her and gave her a quick hard hug in return. "Besides, you'll notice I'm not automatically giving Eli the contract. I'm seriously considering Dean Construction. That's why Nicholas is here tonight—to see how he fits in with our family and friends."

"He seems to be doing just fine," Frankie told him, knowing Harry considered business a family matter.

"Yes, he does." Harry's gaze rested on Nicholas for

a moment. "He'd make a good husband for some lucky woman," he commented guilelessly.

"Hmm," Frankie responded, distracted as Ava, Justin and Lily's daughter, ran across the room and threw herself at Eli. Eli laughed, swinging the little girl high in the air before settling her on his hip. Ava cupped his face in her little hands and gave him an enthusiastic kiss. Eli's eyes sparkled with amusement and his mouth curved in a grin, white teeth flashing in his tanned face. Distracted and charmed by the unabashed affection between the big, undeniably handsome man and the dainty, feminine little girl, it was a moment before Frankie registered Harry's last words. Her gaze snapped to his face. He was eyeing her with an all-too-familiar expression. She nearly groaned aloud. *Oh, no. Surely he's not matchmaking again—and with me and Nicholas Dean?*

She lowered her lashes and hoped her expression didn't give away her suspicions as her mind raced, considering the possibility that Harry had turned his penchant for meddling on her.

"Nicholas has what a woman should be looking for in a husband," Harry continued. "He's proven he's dedicated to business, so he'll be a good provider. Plus, he's young enough to have children but old enough to be a settled father."

Frankie blinked, staring at Harry. "You think that's all a woman wants in a husband? How did you arrive at this abbreviated list?"

Harry waved a hand dismissively. "I covered the essentials. If a woman wants romance, then I suppose

Nicholas qualifies in that department—he's not a bad-looking guy."

"Harry, you're astounding." Frankie leaned closer, gripping his lapel and staring into his eyes. "You left out something extremely important."

"What's that?" Harry's deep voice rumbled, his voice suspicious, as if he was bracing for a blistering lecture.

"You left out the all important x-factor."

His eyebrows lifted. "The x-factor? I've never heard of it."

"Some people call it chemistry. Some call it sexual attraction. I call it the x-factor." *And Eli has it in spades.* The thought flashed through her mind, startling her.

"And you think Nicholas doesn't have it?" Harry sounded skeptical.

"I don't know," Frankie admitted. "I've never been out with him. I was speaking in general terms about women and men."

"Then you're conceding you might be attracted to Nicholas Dean," Harry said shrewdly.

"No." Frankie let go of Harry's lapel and shook her head, exasperated. Over the last few months, she'd successfully ducked Harry's attempts to meddle in her love life, but her sisters Tommi and Bobbie hadn't been as lucky. Fortunately, they'd managed to meet and fall in love with wonderful men on their own, despite Harry's interference. There was no guarantee Frankie would be as lucky, however. She did *not* want Harry focused on finding a husband for her. The very thought was enough to make her shudder and break out in hives. "And we're not talking about Nicholas and me—there *is no* Nicholas and me," she stressed.

"But there could be," Harry insisted. "As soon as his company was shortlisted for HuntCom's south Seattle construction, I had the usual background check run. Which is why I know Dean Construction badly wants to win the contract. I'm dead sure Nicholas will cooperate in getting to know you—and you can find out if the two of you are attracted to each other."

"Harry," Frankie said with forced calm. "I am *not* going to date Nicholas Dean. I don't need my uncle's help in finding men."

"It's not as if I'm out there tracking down men for you, Frankie," Harry protested. "But—"

"Good," Frankie interrupted. "Because if I thought you were trolling Seattle looking for men you can coerce into dating me, I'd go hire a hit man and give him your address."

"Frankie!" Harry looked shocked, but his eyes twinkled. "That's a terrible thing to say. What would your mother think of her favorite daughter threatening my life?"

"She's used to you, Uncle Harry," Frankie said dryly. "She'd probably just ask me what you'd done this time to deserve it."

Harry threw back his head and roared with laughter.

Harry's booming laugh drew everyone's attention. Eli Wolf looked up, over the top of Ava's dark curls and across the room at Frankie Fairchild. She sipped white wine from a stemmed glass, her thick-lashed brown eyes fixed on Harry, an amused smile curving her lips. She was tall at five-eight, with long legs and curves that made a man's hands itch to stroke her. Caramel-blond hair fell to her shoulders in a sleek curtain, framing her beautiful face. The simple, clean-cut lines of a black cocktail dress clung to her body, the long sleeves ending at her wrists. The dress hem was just above her knees, drawing the eye to sleek calves and the delicate bones of her ankles above black pumps with impossibly high heels.

Eli wondered how women walked in those things.

He'd known Francesca Fairchild since she was a little girl. Also, her cousin Justin was his best friend. Unfortunately, those two facts meant Frankie was strictly off-limits for all the things he'd like to do with her—something he'd regretted more often than he cared to think about. Especially over the past four months—ever since that unforgettable kiss at her birthday party.

"Unca Eli?" Ava's small hand tugged his face around until she could meet his gaze. "Mommy says I can have a pet bunny, but first we have to get a cage for him. Will you make one for me? And can I come visit and help you hammer the nails and boards when you make it?"

Eli grinned, glad to be distracted from thoughts of Frankie and charmed as always by the little girl's green eyes and hopeful smile. "Sure, honey. Let's go ask your mom and dad when we can do that."

With Ava perched on his hip, Eli strode across the room to join her parents and settle into a leather armchair. The seat gave him an unobstructed view of Frankie and was placed at right angles to the sofa where Justin and Lily chatted with Cornelia Fairchild, Frankie's mother.

"Mommy." Ava's clear voice piped up. "Unca Eli's going to help me build a bunny house."

"That's wonderful, honey." Lily's rueful gaze met Eli's. "And how does Uncle Eli feel about this?"

"We have a plan," Eli told her with a grin. "And it includes Justin's barbecuing steaks for my granddad to pay my carpenter fee."

"What? How did I get caught up in this?" Justin demanded, his eyes amused.

"Hey, you're the dad," Eli told him with a shrug. "I'm just the uncle."

"I love you, Unca Eli." Ava wrapped her arms around his neck and gave him an enthusiastic kiss on the cheek.

"I love you, too." Eli barely had time to register the swell of affection that filled him before the little girl jumped off his lap and climbed onto her father's. Both Justin and Lily received hugs and kisses, the adults exchanging amused looks.

Ava launched into an excited description of plans for the rabbit hutch.

Only half-listening, Eli leaned back in the comfortable chair, his gaze going past the trio and across the room, drawn inexorably to Frankie once again.

The interplay between her and Harry as they conversed held the ease of comfortable familiarity. Frankie's smile was affectionate as she smiled up at Harry, whose black hair and shrewd eyes, hidden behind dark-framed glasses, belied his age. Eli knew Frankie's father had died when she was a child and if one could judge by appearances, it seemed Harry had stepped in to fill the role.

We have that in common, except it was my grandfather who took over my father's role, Eli mused. *And Frankie still has her mom while I lost both parents.*

Cornelia was a force to be reckoned with, Eli thought, glancing at the older woman's serene face as she listened to Ava describe her rabbit.

But then, so was Jack Wolf. Eli's grandfather had taken in Eli and his three brothers, Conner, Ethan and Matt, a short two hours after a car crash on Seattle's I-5 had taken their parents' lives. Already a widower, Jack became a substitute parent to the four grieving boys, and his fierce commitment and support had created a family to heal their shattered lives.

Frankie watched Eli and Ava cross the room to join Justin and Lily, the little girl waving her hands excitedly as she talked.

"Why are you so determined to fix me up with Nicholas?" she demanded in an attempt to distract Harry, gesturing with her glass. "What about Eli? He's single, he and his brothers own a successful construction company—isn't he on your list of potential suitors?"

Harry glanced over his shoulder. "I'd be happy if you dated Eli. I like the boy," he told her. "But he shows no signs of wanting to settle down. I suspect he's a confirmed bachelor—I doubt he'll ever marry."

"You felt the same way about Justin once," Frankie reminded him. "And look at him now—devoted father, loving husband. He's a contented, happy man since he married Lily."

"True," Harry conceded with a dismissive shrug. "But Eli's different than Justin. Justin hadn't dated for a year or more before he and Lily got back together. He clearly needed Lily and wanted a wife and family. But like I said, Eli's never given the slightest indication of being ready to settle down." He nodded in Nicholas's direction. "Now, you take Nicholas—he seems much more the type to marry and start a family."

Frankie only half listened as Harry continued to list Nicholas Dean's virtues. Unfortunately, she had to agree with Harry about Eli. He'd spent most of the last year recovering in stages after an accident on a construction site that snapped the bone in his lower left leg. Prior to that, however, if rumor was true, he'd been perfectly happy running his company and dating a variety of women. He'd been the poster boy for the quintessential bachelor before his accident, and Frankie assumed he'd returned to his active dating life now that he was recovered.

Wait a minute. Her eyes narrowed with sudden insight. The only way she could convince Harry to scratch her off his list of unmarried family members in need of his matchmaking assistance was if she could make him believe she was in a serious relationship.

But she wasn't dating anyone at the moment, let alone deeply involved. What she needed, she realized, was a man willing to conspire with her to foil Harry. A man who, like her, had something to gain from plotting against her uncle. And a man who had no interest in settling down.

Eli Wolf was *exactly* the kind of man she needed.

She glanced sideways at Harry, murmuring a noncommittal response as he listed the charities that Nicholas Dean had contributed to the prior year.

The question was, would Eli be willing to plot with her to trick Harry?

"…and Nicholas said his family has lived in Queen Anne for over a hundred years," Harry's deep voice recited.

"Interesting," Frankie murmured, catching only the end of Harry's comment.

"Both of his grandmothers are alive," Harry continued, "and live within a few blocks of each other on prime pieces of real estate."

Harry kept talking, but Frankie tuned him out as she considered Harry's matchmaking and how to stop him. She cherished her independence, loved her job as a research assistant and substitute English-literature professor at the University of Washington, and had no interest in changing her life. She was happy, content and did *not* want Harry nudging her toward marriage, no matter how well-intentioned his efforts.

Once again, her gaze went across the room, unerringly zeroing in on Eli. He and Ava were now seated with Lily and Cornelia, the little girl perched on his knee as she waved her hands and chattered enthusiastically to her mother.

Eli Wolf was the only man she knew who could stop Harry's plans. He was well liked by Harry; in fact, he was practically an adopted son. And his company would benefit by getting the contract for constructing the HuntCom campus, so he, too, would benefit from joining forces with her.

An hour later, Frankie was still mulling over the potential scheme as she drove home. It wasn't until she was in her pajamas and in bed, a book opened and then ignored on her lap, that she faced another, potentially more important, issue.

If Eli agreed to help her, they would have to spend time together pretending to be a couple. And maybe— just maybe—she would finally get over her long-ago crush on him.

She'd known Eli since she was eleven years old and her cousin Justin had brought his best friend to a party at Harry's house. When she was fifteen, he'd joined Justin in vetting and harassing her first boyfriends, all under the guise of being protective stand-in brothers.

At sixteen, she'd suffered through a major crush on Eli, who was then twenty-one. By the time she was nineteen, she'd believed her crush was behind her and was relieved she'd kept her feelings a secret. She hadn't even told her three sisters, Georgie, Tommi and Bobbie, about it.

She'd thought yearning after Eli Wolf was a part of her childish, romantic past, her feelings packed away with other high school memories. She'd gone on to date college boys and, later, a fellow professor at the University of Washington, a CPA and a lawyer or two.

She frowned at the blurred lines of type in the open book, not seeing the words.

Until he'd kissed her to wish her happy birthday, she'd been so sure she was over her crush. But the kissing experiment with three other men had raised serious questions.

Surely it couldn't be that Eli Wolf's kisses were addictive and had resurrected her schoolgirl infatuation—but if not, why did other men's lips taste bland and boring?

She needed an answer. She didn't date often, preferring instead to have a mixed circle of friends who attended events in a group. But in her admittedly limited experience, she'd never yet met a man who could hold her interest longer than a few dates. Surely the same thing would happen with Eli—and she'd permanently set aside her childish adoration for him and move on to happily date other men.

But what if she fell for him, rather than growing tired of him?

That won't happen, she scoffed silently as she closed her book, set it on the nightstand and snapped off the lamp. *I'm not foolish enough to fall in love with a commitment-phobic bachelor.*

But she'd have to be on guard, she thought sleepily. She liked her life just as it was. She didn't want to fall in love and surrender her independence or change the basics of her comfortable life. Though twenty years had passed since her father's death, she vividly remembered the following days and months and how devastated her mother had been. Watching her mother over those early years as she coped with grief, Frankie had come to believe that loving deeply carried the potential for even deeper hurt.

Because Cornelia, Frankie and her sisters had adored George Fairchild. It wasn't until after his death that they'd learned he'd had a gambling habit that left his grieving family nearly destitute.

She'd trusted her father with all the blind faith of a child. While she hadn't stopped loving him, as she grew older she'd sworn never to foolishly trust a man that deeply again.

She'd always been goal-oriented and focused, she thought, stifling a yawn. Surely she could be the same while dealing with Eli? She'd keep her eyes on the prize—derailing Harry's matchmaking intentions and putting to rest forever any remnants of her teenage crush.

Satisfied she'd fully considered and understood both the upside and downside of her plan, Frankie fell asleep.

She dreamed of a tall, broad-shouldered man with

black hair and smoky-blue eyes—he held out his arms and her dream self ran joyously toward him.

In her quiet bedroom, she tossed and turned, murmuring and tangling the blankets as she dreamed.

Chapter Two

Two days after dinner at Harry's house, Frankie left her office on the University of Washington campus midmorning and drove to Ballard. The Seattle community was twenty minutes west of the UW campus and an equal distance northwest of downtown Seattle. Wolf Construction's business office was located in the industrial section near the Ballard Locks. Except for a diesel pickup truck with a Wolf Construction logo on the door, the parking lot on the south side of the building was empty.

When she entered the outer office, the reception area was quiet and empty, the two secretarial desks vacant.

"Hello?" No one answered her call, and she frowned. Surely the office's outer door would have been locked if no one was here?

The silence was broken by a loud thump somewhere deeper in the building, followed by a male voice muttering what sounded like swearing. Frankie peered past the desks and down the hallway beyond, where several doors stood open into offices.

"Hello?" she called again. When no one appeared, Frankie waited another moment before determinedly rounding the desk and marching down the hall.

"Damn it," a male voice rumbled with annoyance. "Where the hell did Connor put those plans?"

Frankie followed the deep voice, stepping into an office. She halted just inside. Eli stood across the room, his back to her as he pulled open a drawer and shuffled through the papers inside. He wore heavy black work boots, jeans and a black T-shirt. He bent over the drawer, and faded denim pulled tight over his rear. Beneath the snug clothes, sculpted muscles shifted and bunched as he stretched to reach the back of the drawer. Frankie stared, riveted, her body heating as her gaze followed the movements of his powerful body.

He straightened, shoving the drawer closed and opening the next one with an impatient jerk.

The noise snapped Frankie out of the spell that held her, and she gathered her composure, taking a deep, calming breath. "Hello, Eli."

He stiffened and quickly swung around, his eyes flaring with surprise just before his mouth curved in a grin.

"Frankie? What are you doing here?"

Now that she was actually about to propose her

plan to Eli, Frankie was suddenly nervous. Her fingers gripped the leather strap of her black Coach purse a bit tighter.

"I need to talk to you about something. Do you have a few minutes?"

Clearly surprised, he cocked his head to the side, considering her for a brief moment. "Sure." He tossed a roll of blueprints into the open drawer, pushed it closed and moved away from the cabinet. "Come on in. Have a seat." He gestured at the two leather armchairs facing the desk. "I'd offer you something to drink, but the office staff has the day off and the coffee is probably cold sludge left over from yesterday."

"Thanks, but I'm fine." Frankie crossed to the chair and sat, perching on the edge of the comfortable seat.

Eli half sat on the edge of the desk facing her. The position had him much too close to her. She had to look up to meet his gaze. At eye level, the worn denim of his jeans stretched across powerful thighs. Determinedly, she kept her gaze on his face.

"So, tell me," he prompted when she hesitated. "What brings you to Ballard this morning?"

Now that she was here, faced with explaining her plan to Eli, Frankie was reluctant to begin the conversation.

"What were you looking for when I came in?" she asked, not answering his question. "You sounded frustrated."

Eli glanced over his shoulder at the cabinet. "Frustrated isn't a strong enough word," he said, his gaze swinging back to meet hers. "My brother Connor told his secretary to send the blueprints down to the job site, but she sent the wrong ones. I came back to pick them up, but I'll be damned if I can find them." He jerked a thumb over his shoulder at the cabinet with its long drawers. "They're not in the project drawer." He sounded thoroughly disgusted.

"Can you call him on his cell and ask him?" Frankie suggested.

"I tried that," he told her. "He's not answering."

"I'm sorry," she said with sympathy. "I know how disturbing it can be to have a project stopped. I hate wasting time while I wait for someone to respond before I can move forward."

He nodded, his blue eyes warming. "It's bloody annoying," he agreed.

Eli studied Frankie through narrowed eyes.

She's nervous, he thought with surprise. Making small talk about his search for the blueprints was only a ruse to delay telling him why she was here.

When he'd swung around and saw her framed in the office doorway, he'd been slammed with the same jolt of awareness that had plagued him ever since they'd shared a kiss at her birthday party four months earlier. Though it was meant to be casual, he hadn't been able to forget the feel and taste of Frankie's soft, lush mouth under his.

She'd featured prominently in more than one hot, sweaty dream ever since, leaving him sleep deprived and cranky the next morning.

He raked his fingers through his hair and shifted, forcing himself to remember the beautiful blonde sitting in the chair facing him was Justin's cousin and, therefore, off-limits. "Come on, Frankie," he coaxed. "Tell me why you're here."

She shifted in her chair, slim fingers tucking a strand of hair behind one small ear. She sat primly, feet aligned on the floor, hands now resting quietly on her lap. "I've known you a long time, Eli," she began. "And more importantly, you've known my uncle Harry since you were a teenager. I'm sure you're aware of Harry's scheme to force his sons to marry, and how Justin fell in love with Lily in spite of Harry's interference."

"Of course." Eli nodded. "Justin told me before the wedding."

"What you might not be aware of," Frankie went on, "is that Harry seems to think that since his scheming to force his sons to marry turned out so well, he's decided to become a matchmaker for the Fairchilds. All four of us—including me."

Eli was stunned. "You're kidding" was all he could manage to get out. He shook his head in disbelief, but Frankie's face didn't look as if this was a joke. "That doesn't make any sense. He damn near ruined all four of his sons' chances at marrying the women they wanted."

"I know!" Frankie leaned forward. "And he almost did the same with Tommi and Bobbie! Apparently, he thinks he's successful, however, because he's turned his sights on me."

"What the hell?" Eli felt as if he'd been punched in the gut. "Who does Harry want you to marry?"

"Nicholas Dean."

Oh, hell no! Eli's rejection of the possibility that Frankie would marry Nicholas Dean was visceral and immediate. Somehow, he kept himself from snarling aloud. "Why did he pick Dean?" he asked, aware his voice was deeper, rougher than it had been only moments before.

Frankie waved one small, graceful hand. "Who knows? I think he picked Nicholas because Dean Construction was on Harry's radar. Harry told me he'd run the usual background check on the company when it was shortlisted for the contract to build HuntCom's new building in south Seattle. Evidently, Harry was impressed with Nicholas's work ethic, plus the fact that he's single, so Harry decided he should encourage Nicholas to ask me out."

"And you're not on board with the plan?"

"No!" Frankie frowned at him, her brown eyes sparking with gold. "I'm not."

"I see." Relief flooded Eli, the corners of his mouth lifting in a grin. "And you want me to tell Harry you're not interested in dating Nicholas?" he guessed.

"I've already told Uncle Harry I'm not interested," she informed him. "It didn't faze him, and I suspect he's working on a scheme to push me and Nicholas together even as we speak."

Eli's smile disappeared.

"I've watched Uncle Harry interfere in Tommi's

and Bobbie's love lives," Frankie went on. "And I'm convinced the only way to stop his matchmaking is to convince him that I'm taken. That's where you come in."

Eli blinked. "That's where I come in?" he repeated.

She nodded decisively. "I have zero interest in getting married—and the general consensus of opinion in the family is that you don't, either. Which makes you the perfect person for my plan."

Eli narrowed his eyes over her thoughtfully. "I'm not sure I'm following you. Maybe you should give me the abbreviated version."

Frankie waved her hands expressively, her expression wry. "I'm sorry—let me back up. The other night at Harry's house when he was telling me all the reasons I should want to date and perhaps marry Nicholas Dean, you were standing across the room holding Ava. I'm afraid I used you to distract Harry and asked him why he didn't suggest you as a potential husband. He told me he doubted you would marry. He said you seemed perfectly happy with your life as it was. Well…" She shrugged. "The moment Harry said that, I realized you were the perfect person for me to date, because neither of us wants to get married. When Harry kept droning on about all of Nicholas's good qualities, I had a brainstorm."

"A brainstorm," Eli repeated. He realized belatedly that he kept repeating her statements and told himself to stop.

"Yes, exactly." She leaned forward, her brown eyes

gleaming with determination. "Which brings me to the reason I came to see you today. I need to convince Harry I'm madly in love and deeply committed to someone so he'll stop trying to pair me up with single men. But I'm not in love, and there's no one on my horizon. So I need someone to *pretend* to be involved with, while you," she continued, pointing at him, "would like Wolf Construction to win the contract for the new HuntCom building. So…my proposal is that we team up. If you'll pretend to be involved with me, I can almost guarantee Uncle Harry will move Wolf Construction to the top of the list for the contract. He's already narrowed it down to you and Nicholas, and he as good as admitted to me that he's inclined to award contracts to family or close family friends."

"You want me to date you in order to get Harry to give my company a contract?" Eli asked, his tone neutral.

"Not exactly," she told him. "I'm only suggesting that we both have something to gain—and frankly, I need a pretend-date/boyfriend as fast as possible. Harry, my mother and sisters already know and adore you, so they won't bat an eye if it's you I claim to have fallen madly in love with. If I introduce someone new, they're going to be more skeptical. I want Harry off my back. Heaven knows what trouble he can stir up for me." She shuddered.

Eli stared at her for a long moment. He didn't want her believing he was the kind of man who would use her to gain a lucrative construction contract. On the other hand, there was no way he'd let her be courted by Nicholas Dean.

Not that Dean was a bad guy. He was, in fact, everything Harry thought he was—smart, successful and played a mean game of pool. Just the kind of man a woman could easily fall in love with.

Which was why there was no way in hell Eli was going to let him near Frankie, not if he could help it. He knew he was being territorial, but he couldn't seem to help it.

Probably because I want to be the one burning up the sheets with Frankie, he thought. In fact, he realized with a start, he'd felt that way for months.

And it was time he did something about it.

"Well," she said expectantly, interrupting his thoughts. "Will you do it?"

"Yeah," he said with a slow drawl. "I will." He stood, bending to cup her elbow and lift her from the chair. "Let's go get some coffee and talk about the details."

He hustled her out of the office and down the street to Zena's Café before she had time to change her mind.

"So," he said when they were seated in a booth with steaming mugs in front of them, "how do you envision going forward with this campaign to fool Harry?"

"I thought we'd keep it simple," Frankie told him. "We can work out a list of events Harry is likely to attend. Then we can appear together and pretend to be in love while Harry's watching. Hopefully, it won't take long to convince him. Once he accepts that, he can cross me off his matchmaking list and sign your company contract for the new HuntCom campus, and we can go back to our normal lives."

"Harry's pretty shrewd—I'm not sure he's going to be as easy to convince as you seem to think," Eli told her. "He didn't get his reputation as a shark in the financial world by being dense."

"But that's business." Frankie propped her forearms on the polished wood tabletop and leaned forward. "When it comes to personal relationships, Harry can be amazingly unaware. Look at the women he married— disasters, every one of them."

"You've got a point." Eli shrugged. "It's hard to argue with his marital record. The only good thing about Harry's ex-wives is that he stopped getting married after making four bad choices."

"Exactly." Frankie nodded decisively. "I truly antici- pate he'll accept our romantic smoke screen as fact. I don't think he'll look deeper."

"Nevertheless," Eli told her. "If we're going to do this, let's do it right. Remember," he cautioned her, "it's not just Harry we have to convince. Your mother or sisters are likely to be attending the same functions as Harry. If we're not believable, they'll never buy it. Cornelia's not going to be easy to fool—especially when it comes to one of her daughters. And if Cornelia knows we're faking, she's likely to tell Harry."

Frankie frowned, unconsciously winding a lock of hair around her forefinger in a gesture Eli had noticed her make before when she was deep in thought.

"You're right," she murmured. She looked up at Eli,

her brown eyes alive with bright determination, gold flecks swimming in the chocolate-brown depths. "So we can't let her know we're pretending. Think you can pull it off?"

Her tone matched the challenge in the quick curve of her lips.

"Absolutely." He lifted a brow, tossing the challenge back at her with a slow smile. "The question is, can you?"

She laughed, shrugging in a quick, elegant shift of her shoulders beneath the tailored blue suit jacket. "A woman learns to fake being interested in a guy before she's out of junior high school. It's a rite of passage."

"Yeah?" Startled and intrigued, Eli lifted an eyebrow in inquiry. "Why in junior high?"

"Because at my school, that was the first year of boy-girl dances, and every girl wanted a date. Unfortunately, the girls outnumbered the boys two-to-one. Which meant there was a lot of competition for invitations to the school functions."

Eli swept a slow, appreciative gaze over her face, hair, down her throat and the swell of her breasts beneath the cream blouse she wore under her suit jacket. The table edge prevented him from going lower, and he returned to meet her eyes. "I bet you never had to compete for a date. I'm guessing the boys were lined up next to your school locker, waiting for you to choose."

She threw back her head and laughed, the throaty musical sound stroking over Eli as if she'd touched him.

"Not hardly," she said when she stopped chuckling,

her eyes dancing. "When I was thirteen, I wore braces, was skinny—straight up and down without a curve in sight—spent most of my time with my nose buried in a book, and last but not least, I was taller than any boy in my class. So, no...I wasn't exactly the most desirable date on anyone's list." She lifted her cup and sipped, eyeing him with amusement.

"No kidding?" Bemused, he stared at her. "I'm trying to imagine you as a skinny thirteen-year-old with crooked teeth, and it just doesn't compute."

"I'll show you one of my seventh-grade class pictures sometime. Trust me—I'm not lying. In fact..." She considered for a moment. "It's entirely possible that the reality of my thirteen-year-old nerdiness was much worse than I'm describing."

Eli laughed, charmed by her candid comments. "Why don't I remember you at thirteen?" he asked.

"Because you and Justin were freshmen in college that year and really busy—I hardly saw Justin that year, except for dinner on Christmas Day," Frankie told him.

"That's right," Eli mused, thinking back. "First year at the UW was crazy busy. Now I wish I'd taken time to visit at Christmas. If I had, I could have seen you in braces."

"You didn't miss much," she said dryly. "How about you? I'm guessing you weren't a skinny nerd with braces when you were thirteen."

Eli considered. "You'd have to ask the girls in my class whether they thought I was a nerd," he told her. "I didn't have braces, but I earned good grades and I was certainly a lot skinnier than I am now."

"I bet you were cute." She sighed. "If you'd been in my class, I'm sure you would have had girls lined up outside your locker." She eyed him with curiosity. "And I bet you have girls lined up outside your condo now. It just occurred to me to wonder—do you have a lady friend who's going to be upset with our pretend love affair?"

He shook his head. "No. If I did, I wouldn't have agreed."

She sipped her coffee and eyed him over the rim. "I know it's none of my business, but after listening to the occasional comment from Justin, I've always assumed you're usually dating someone. I'm glad you're currently available, because it certainly makes my plan to fool Uncle Harry much easier, but why are you unattached?"

Eli didn't want to tell her that even if he'd been dating someone, he would have untangled himself immediately. There was no way he'd let Harry maneuver her into dating and maybe marrying Nicholas Dean. He didn't want to look too closely at the reasons he felt so strongly about Frankie dating Dean, but he accepted that he did.

"I suppose the truth is, I haven't had time to think about dating lately. I've only been back at work full-time for a couple of months."

"Oh, that's right." Her brown eyes warmed with sympathy. "I knew you were hurt at work last year, but I hadn't realized you'd only recently recovered."

"It took a while," he said. "I fell off a scaffold on a construction site and broke my left leg." He shrugged. "It was a clean break, but there were complications requiring two more surgeries—I was housebound and unable to work most of the year. Plus, I was in physical therapy off and on for months. The end result was that I was rarely in the office—or anywhere else, for that matter," he added. "Practically the only social function I went to that year was your birthday party at Harry's house. I was between surgeries that month."

Her lashes lowered, screening her eyes, and faint color tinted her fair skin. "No wonder you aren't involved with someone at the moment," she said, lifting her gaze to his once more. "You haven't had time."

"No." He pretended not to notice she'd avoided commenting about her birthday party but knew from the color in her cheeks that she hadn't forgotten that kiss any more than he had. "The worst part was the boredom. I have no patience with sitting around. A guy can only watch so many cable-TV sports events without a break. Thank God I'm fully recovered and back at work, because, trust me—my grandfather and brothers were about ready to throw me into Puget Sound and let me drown."

She laughed, her eyes sparkling with amusement. "I'm sure you couldn't have been that difficult."

"According to them, I was worse," he assured her. "I'm not a good patient—in fact, I'm lousy at it." Maybe that was the reason he was so eager to take up Frankie's plan to foil Harry, Eli thought. Maybe the memory of those long, boring months had made him susceptible to any pretty woman with an interesting scheme. "Your plan to outmaneuver Harry at his own game is perfect timing for me," he told her, although he suspected Frankie was the most compelling element. "It's just intriguing enough to distract me and make me forget those never-ending months of being stuck at home with my leg in a cast."

"Whatever it is that made you agree, I'm just thankful you've said yes." Frankie smiled at him and slid the tip of her tongue over the plump curve of her lower lip, licking away a drop of creamy coffee. Eli nearly groaned out loud, his body tensing.

He saw women drinking coffee nearly every morning when he stopped at the local Starbucks on his way to work. He didn't have this reaction to any of them, he realized with a flash of awareness. Only Frankie managed to turn him on with one glimpse of the tip of her tongue sliding slowly over her bottom lip.

No, it's not just any woman I want. It's Frankie.

Chapter Three

Frankie glanced up just in time to see Eli's lashes lower, his eyes going dark as he stared at her mouth.

She'd certainly seen desire on a man's face before. But Eli's intent, focused stare sent heat shivering through her belly. She felt her cheeks warming and knew her face must be flushing with pink color.

She was speechless, unable to respond as she watched Eli's dark gaze flick upward to hers, awareness arcing between them in a palpable hum.

Fortunately, he apparently took pity on her frozen vocal chords. His mouth curved in a warm smile.

"When do you want to start our scam?" he asked mildly, with no trace of the heat that had flared between them. "Soon?"

"The sooner the better," she told him, happy to set

aside contemplation of that moment between them until she was alone. "Especially if you're right about Harry not being convinced quickly or easily."

"This is one time when I hope I'm wrong, but knowing Harry, I doubt it," Eli said wryly. "That only makes the challenge more interesting, though." He winked at her, a gleam of anticipation in his blue eyes. "Do you have a plan?"

"I thought we'd start with a simple, first-date kind of thing. Mom has tickets to a fundraiser for the Children's Hospital on Saturday night—she said a group of her friends are going together, including Harry."

"Sounds good. What time shall I pick you up?"

"Around eight—and it's black tie," she added.

"I think Connor mentioned he's taking someone," Eli commented. "It's a dinner dance, right?"

Frankie nodded.

"Do you think Cornelia can wangle seats for us at her table? I'm assuming Harry will be sitting with her."

"He almost always does if they're at the same function. I'll ask her to pull strings so we can join them." Frankie glanced at her wristwatch and gasped. "Oh, no. Look at the time. I'm going to be late for my next class." She caught up her purse and slid out of the booth, only to find Eli already standing.

He pulled a handful of bills out of his pocket and peeled off several, dropping them on the table before cupping her elbow in his warm palm. "Let's go."

They moved quickly down the sidewalk and back to the Wolf Construction parking lot; Eli tucked a card with his home and cell-phone numbers into her jacket pocket as they walked. Frankie recited her home address and phone numbers, impressed when he didn't need to write them down.

At five-eight, Frankie had never considered herself dainty but walking next to Eli made her feel delicate and very feminine. He was not only much taller, he was broader, bulkier and outweighed her by what must surely be at least a hundred pounds. Additionally, he exuded a protectiveness that made her feel safe. Cherished.

He handed her into her car, bending to say he'd see her on Saturday night. As she drove away from the lot, she glanced in her rearview mirror. He stood motionless, hands shoved into the front pockets of his jeans, the faint breeze ruffling his dark hair as he watched her leave.

She wondered briefly if she'd made a mistake. She wanted to put a stop to Harry's matchmaking so she could go on with her life, unimpeded by marriage-minded suitors. She'd purposely picked Eli because she was convinced he had as little interest in matrimony as she did.

But after spending more than an hour in his company, she was having second thoughts.

Not about Eli—about herself. She was definitely attracted to him. Could she keep that attraction from complicating their plan to distract Harry?

She narrowed her eyes thoughtfully as she left Ballard and headed back to the university campus.

Of course I can, she concluded after several moments.

Granted, Eli Wolf has the power to send my hormones crazy, but that doesn't mean I have to act on the feeling.

She'd remain levelheaded and keep the end goal in mind, she decided firmly. Eli would only become a problem for her if she allowed him to distract her. She just had to remember that he wasn't a man interested in a long-term relationship—that irrefutable fact should be enough to keep her from falling foolishly in love with him.

Braking for a stoplight, she used her cell phone's speaker feature. "Mom? I'm so glad I caught you—can you get me two tickets for the fundraiser on Saturday night? And can we join your table?" She paused. "Yes, Mom, I'm bringing a date. Oops, have to go—I'm driving back to campus and the light just changed. See you Saturday!"

Later that evening after showering and donning pajama bottoms and a pink tank top, Frankie brewed a cup of green tea and climbed into bed. She loved her bedroom—it was her favorite room in her Queen Anne condo. Aided by her sisters, she'd painted three of the walls in a buttery cream color, but the fourth was a warm shade of red-gold pumpkin. Her bedstead was antique mahogany and had a matching nightstand. After months of searching, she'd found a tall chest of drawers that nearly matched the bed at an antique shop in Greenwood.

The lamp on her nightstand was a rare antique Tiffany,

a Christmas gift from Uncle Harry, while the fluffy white comforter that covered the bed's wide mattress had been a birthday gift from her mother.

In a corner near the window, a huge Boston fern sat atop a tall wicker floor stand, just to the left of a low base holding a medium-sized TV, its plasma screen now dark.

Frankie plumped the pillows and tucked them against the headboard behind her, then picked up the remote control and switched on the television. The eleven o'clock news was airing video of local trash collectors' union members marching outside city hall with picket signs. The mayor's comments on the status of union negotiations accompanied the video.

Frankie leaned back and sipped her tea as her thoughts drifted to her meeting with Eli that morning.

After spending time alone with him, she certainly understood how he'd earned a reputation as a man adored by women. No wonder he was reputed to date a lot. He was undeniably handsome, but there was something else, some indefinable element that made a woman feel as if she were the only female in the room. When he'd stared at her mouth, his eyes going dark, she'd felt the intensity of his gaze as if he'd reached out and touched her.

She shivered. This morning's encounter with Eli had erased any doubts—she was still attracted to him. And that scared her.

Frowning, she sipped her tea and pondered why that should be. She'd dated off and on since she was sixteen;

she'd known Eli longer than that. She wasn't afraid of him in any rational way.

And yet, she was wary on some deep, primal level.

But wouldn't any reasonable woman be cautious of a man who could break her heart?

No. She instantly rejected the possibility he could break her heart. *I had a schoolgirl crush on him. That's the only reason I'm feeling this way. I can't possibly be in love with him, therefore, he can't break my heart.*

She was twenty-nine years old, not sixteen, she told herself. And she was eminently practical and well educated, having earned a doctorate in English lit, a master's degree in mathematics and a second master's degree in science. She was light-years away from that foolish sixteen-year-old who had dreamed about Eli Wolf.

But maybe the timing was wrong back then, a small voice said. And maybe now, with Eli unattached and you available, too, the stars are aligned and the time is right.

Frankie ignored the voice, burying it under a determined analysis of the details of the plan to fool Harry.

Yes, she thought firmly, *this will work. I just have to remember we're both playing a part, pretending to be attracted to each other.*

Unbidden, the memory of his eyes staring at her mouth swept over her.

Pretending to be attracted to Eli wasn't going to be the problem, Frankie realized. The real problem might very well be convincing herself *not* to truly fall for him.

* * *

Saturday dawned wet and chilly. The sky over Seattle was gray and lowering, the clouds seeming to hover around the top of the Space Needle. Rain fell intermittently, but the weather cleared late in the afternoon, giving Frankie hope that the evening might be nicer.

Before heading for the shower prior to her date with Eli, Frankie selected a small emerald green envelope purse from a chest drawer. She tucked the two tickets to tonight's fundraiser, a condo key, lipstick, a twenty-dollar bill for emergencies and several tissues into the bag. Then she slid her favorite evening coat from its padded hanger in her bedroom closet and carried both items into the living room, dropping the purse onto the seat of an upholstered wing chair and draping the coat over the back. The long black coat reached almost to her ankles and, with its round collar and loose sleeves, was perfect for protecting an evening gown from the winter wind and rain.

Back in her bedroom, she laid out underwear and chose a pair of black stiletto heels to pair with her gown. A half hour later, fresh from her shower, she smoothed scented lotion over her skin and slipped into a lacy strapless bra with matching celery-green bikini panties and garter belt.

Justin's wife, Lily, was a lingerie designer and kept Frankie in fabulous underwear. Everything feminine within her delighted in the silk and lace creations—in fact, walking into Lily's shop, Princess Lily's Boutique, in Ballard, never failed to make her smile with delight.

She sat on the edge of the bed to carefully don sheer, delicate stockings before stepping into her dress. The emerald-green satin gown was strapless, with a zipper up the back. The bodice was snug, fitted to closely follow the outward curve of her breasts and inward curve of the narrow waist. A wide band of crystal beading in glittering jet black covered the upper edge of the bodice.

Frankie slipped into her shoes, fastening the narrow black straps around her ankles, and rose to cross to the antique mirror standing next to the closet doors. She twisted to look at the zipper closure, checking to ensure it was fastened, then took jet black drop earrings with their matching necklace and bracelet from the jewelry case atop the high chest. It was the work of a few moments to fasten the earrings and bracelet, but the necklace clasp was difficult. After several tries, Frankie left the room with the gold-set jet beads cradled in one hand, switching on the bedside lamp as she went.

The doorbell rang just as she entered the living room, and a quick glance out the peephole revealed Eli in the hallway outside. He wore a classic black tuxedo, the white collar of his shirt a sharp contrast against the tanned skin of his throat. He stood with casual ease, his hands tucked into the pockets of his slacks.

The quick little zing of anticipation that sent her heart racing wasn't quite as startling this time. Maybe she was simply growing accustomed to the increase in heartbeat and the adrenaline rush she felt each time she saw him, she thought. She slipped the dead bolt free and pulled the door open.

"Hi, Eli. Come in—I'll just be a moment."

"Hey," he said lazily, his gaze slowly moving over her face, hair, and lower to her toes before returning to meet hers once again. Male appreciation heated his blue eyes. "You look great. I like the dress."

Frankie's toes curled in her black stilettos, and the heat that arced between them had her lowering her eyes from his and turning away to a small oval mirror. The glass hung on the wall next to the coat closet, only feet from the door.

"Thank you. I won't be long—I just have to fasten my necklace." She frowned at the clasp. It wasn't the usual hook and eye, nor did it have a sliding lock. The mechanism was one Frankie hadn't seen before.

"Problems?" Eli asked, walking closer.

"I'm not sure how to close this clasp." She held up the necklace, narrowing her eyes over it. "It belonged to my great-aunt Francine. This is the first time I've worn it, and I've never seen a fastening quite like this."

"May I?" He held out his hand, and Frankie dropped the web of gold-set jet beads into his palm.

He lifted the necklace, the delicate feminine settings dangling from his calloused fingers as he inspected the lock.

"I think I've got it. Turn around and hold up your hair."

Frankie obeyed, waiting until he draped the necklace

around her throat before she bent her head and lifted her hair up and away from her nape. The mirror on the wall allowed her to see his frown of concentration as he bent his head. The backs of his fingers brushed against her skin as he fastened the intricate clasp. Each warm touch heightened her senses, making her vividly aware of his taller, broader body only inches from hers. Her heart beat faster, her breathing shallower and more swift.

"Done," he said with satisfaction. He looked up, his gaze unerringly finding hers in the mirror's reflection.

Frankie caught her breath. For one long moment, time slowed.

Heat flared in his eyes, the curve of his mouth suddenly sensual, fuller. Frankie's heart fluttered wildly. She was suddenly unsure how she would react if he turned her into his arms and kissed her as he had in her dreams.

Then his thick lashes lowered, effectively screening his eyes. He stepped back, and the spell was broken as he turned to lift her coat from the nearby chair.

He held the black evening wrap, and, wordlessly, she slipped her arms into the sleeves. His hands rested lightly on her shoulders for a brief, electric moment before he handed her the tiny green purse from the chair's cushion.

"Got everything?" he asked as she turned toward the door.

"Yes." She smiled up at him, determined to match his cool calm.

They left the condo, chatting about the weather as they rode downstairs in the elevator to the quiet lobby.

A long, black limousine stood at the curb, and Frankie had barely cleared the lobby's doorway when the driver appeared to pull open the back door.

Eli cupped her elbow and hurried her across the sidewalk to tuck her into the backseat, sliding in behind her. The door closed smoothly, sealing them into the warm, dry, leather-scented interior.

"How lovely to have curb service," Frankie said with appreciation. "Especially since it's started raining again."

"Not to mention the driver is the one who'll have to negotiate the traffic downtown," Eli added dryly.

"Yes, that, too." Frankie nodded. "Very wise of you not to drive tonight."

Eli stretched out his long legs. "I would have driven, but my Porsche is in the shop and I didn't want to pick you up in my work truck." He grinned, amusement in his eyes. "I'd hate to get grease on that pretty dress you're wearing."

"Good call." Her voice was dry. "You should have told me about your car. I would have been happy to pick you up."

He lifted an eyebrow in pretend shock. "And risk having my grandfather find out I'd made a date and had the lady drive me?" He shuddered. "I'd rather be caught running naked on Denny Way. He'd never let me forget it."

Frankie laughed. "Your grandfather sounds like fun."

"He is," Eli answered promptly. "Don't get me wrong—I love the old guy. If he hadn't taken me and my brothers in after our folks were killed, we might have been split up and sent into foster homes. But he still thinks he should meddle in our lives, just like he did when we were kids."

"And you can't tell him to butt out, because you love him and don't want to hurt his feelings," Frankie guessed aloud.

"Exactly." Eli looked at her, his gaze searching her face. "How did you know?"

"Because that's how I feel about Uncle Harry," she replied. "I adore him, but he's got to stop interfering in my life." She shrugged. "Oh, I know we're both adults and I could just tell him to stop. I could be blunt and tell him I hate knowing he's actively trying to dragoon men into dating me, as if no guy would ever think of asking me out unless Harry strong-armed them." She lifted her hands in frustration, then let them drop to her lap. "But I know he'd be hurt, so I don't say the words. Which is why I came up with this scheme." She gestured between Eli and herself. "You and me."

"If Harry finds out you're trying to trick him, he'll be hurt anyway," Eli cautioned her.

"I know." Her mouth drooped. She glanced sideways and found him watching her with an oddly tender expression. "Which is why we have to be very convincing," she said firmly.

"Agreed." The car slowed, and he glanced out the window. "Here's the hotel—put on your best I'm-so-in-love acting face, honey, because the curtain is about to go up."

Chapter Four

The Grand Sylvania's portico roof shielded the car from the rain as Eli stepped out and turned to take Frankie's hand. The well-lit area did nothing to hold the wind at bay, however, and the two hurried into the hotel lobby, joining other guests to ride an escalator to the second floor. The muted rumble of crowd laughter and conversation underlaid an orchestra's rendition of a Broadway tune as they stepped off the moving stairs and neared an open ballroom door.

A hotel employee greeted them, taking Frankie's coat before passing it on to a young woman in a white evening gown, a Children's Hospital ribbon pinned to her bodice.

"May I have your tickets, please?"

Frankie quickly located the lavender cards in her small evening purse and handed them over.

"Ah, yes. This way, please."

"Thank you." Frankie smiled at their hostess and followed her. Close behind her, Eli's hand rested on the curve of her waist, his palm and long fingers warm and faintly possessive. Frankie was vibrantly aware of his broad bulk at her back; the very air separating them seemed alive with electricity.

They wound their way between tables toward the front of the big room. Frankie scanned the guests, locating Cornelia seated with Harry and another couple at a table for six on the edge of the polished dance floor.

Cornelia looked up, her lips curving in a welcoming smile as she raised a hand to beckon with a wave. Then her gaze moved past Frankie, her eyes widening as she saw Eli. She quickly looked back at Frankie, her eyebrows lifting in silent query just as the two reached the table.

"Hello, Mother." Frankie bent to kiss Cornelia's cheek and paused to say hello to Marcia Adkins.

Harry and Jonathon Adkins stood, greeting Frankie and Eli as he drew out a chair for her. She murmured her thanks, smoothing her skirts as Eli settled into the chair next to her.

"I didn't know you were bringing Eli," Cornelia said with a smile. "But I'm glad you did. It's lovely to see you, Eli. I hardly got to say more than hello to you the other evening at Harry's house."

"I'm sorry, Cornelia. Justin and Lily promised Ava

she could have a pet rabbit for her birthday. We spent most of the evening discussing the proper size of the hutch we're going to build." Eli's eyes twinkled.

"That's my Ava," Harry said with a fond pride. "You'll notice she went straight to a professional builder," he said to Jonathon.

"Not to mention choosing a man most likely to give her whatever she wants," Eli said dryly, earning him a soft, approving smile from Cornelia.

"You've got competition for the title," Harry told him. "From her dad, me and her three uncles."

Eli laughed. "True. She's a charmer, that little girl." He turned to speak with a waiter, and Cornelia leaned close to murmur in Frankie's ear.

"You didn't tell me Eli was your date for tonight."

"It was a last-minute thing," Frankie whispered back.

"I didn't realize you two were dating." Cornelia's comment held a question.

"We've seen each other a few times," Frankie said. It wasn't really a lie, she told herself. She and Eli *had* seen each other recently—once at Harry's house and then again at his office. That qualified as seeing each other, didn't it?

Cornelia's expression was intrigued, but before she could question Frankie further, two waiters arrived with bottles of champagne and began pouring.

"Oh, how wonderful. I love champagne," Frankie said with delight, accepting a flute from Eli. "How did you know?"

"You had champagne at your last birthday party."

His gaze met hers, and Frankie's heart skipped a beat. The memory of her birthday party and the kiss they'd shared was in his eyes, and Frankie was suddenly back there, his mouth on hers, his arms warm and hard, wrapping her tight against the powerful muscles of his chest and thighs....

"How nice that you remembered."

Cornelia's warm voice broke the spell that held Frankie, and she tore her gaze from Eli's, looking down at the bubbles rising in the gold liquid filling her flute.

Eli relaxed in his chair, a glass in one hand, the other arm stretched out along the back of Frankie's chair. His fingers brushed the bare curve of her shoulder before closing warmly, lightly, over the nape of her neck.

"I remember everything about Frankie." His voice was deeper, huskier.

Frankie glanced sideways, and their gazes meshed. She tried to remember he was only playing a role. But his blue eyes were darker, smokier, and the heat within seemed so real Frankie felt herself melting, her body unconsciously softening, easing toward his.

"I don't recall seeing you at Frankie's last birthday party," Harry said.

Frankie glanced up, alerted by Harry's tone, and saw his eyes narrow over Eli.

"I wasn't there long," Eli said without missing a beat. "I'd barely recovered from a second leg surgery and stopped in for a few minutes, looking for Justin. I didn't know you were having a party until I got there and only stayed long enough to say hello and toast the birthday girl before leaving."

"Ah, that must be why I don't remember—I probably didn't see you in the crowd," Harry mused.

"There were a lot of people at the house," Eli agreed.

His fingertips absently stroked the curve of Frankie's shoulder, almost as if he was savoring the tactile pleasure of her skin against his. Despite knowing he was only touching her because Harry and Cornelia were watching, Frankie still shivered inwardly, her skin heating beneath his touch.

"Oh, Jonathon," Marcia exclaimed, her eyes lighting as the orchestra played the opening notes of a classic Burt Bacharach tune. "I love this song—come dance with me." She held out her hand to her husband.

"Excuse us, folks," Jonathon said as he rose and took his wife's hand.

Eli leaned closer, his lips brushing Frankie's earlobe.

"Let's dance."

She nodded silently, and he stood, pulling back her chair.

"Harry, you should dance with Mom," she said as Eli took her hand, threading her fingers through his.

"I think we'll sit this one out and finish our champagne," Harry replied.

Frankie thought she caught a fleeting frown cross

her mother's features before Eli tugged her gently out onto the gleaming floor.

He turned her into his arms, tucking her close. Her temple rested against his cheek, and each breath she took drew in the subtle scent of his aftershave, warmed by body heat. She loved that smell, she thought, leaning closer.

"Did you see Harry's face?" Eli's voice was a low rumble. He chuckled, his breath ghosting against her ear. "He can't decide whether to demand we tell him why we're here together or pretend it's not happening."

Frankie laughed. "I'd give anything to hear what he's saying to Mom right now."

Eli's arms tightened around Frankie. "Heads up," he whispered in her ear. "Harry and your mom are heading this way."

Frankie tilted her head back and looked up at him. "Do we have a plan?" she asked, even as she reveled in the muscled strength of his arm at her waist, his warm fingers threaded through hers and the press of her increasingly sensitized body as it lay against his from breast to thigh.

His lashes lowered, his eyes going darker as the moment stretched. Then he swung her in a slow circle, his steps sure as he swept her into a secluded corner, behind a tall column with baskets of ferns and flowers widening its base.

Her skirts swirled around his legs as he stopped, easing her backward against the column's support.

His gaze didn't leave hers as he bent his head and brushed his mouth against hers.

It was like touching a live electrical wire. Frankie started, her hands curling into fists over his lapels as she caught her breath.

"Shh," he murmured against her lips. Then his mouth fitted carefully over hers, changing the angle of the kiss as it lengthened, stealing the oxygen from her lungs until he breathed for her.

Frankie forgot that a roomful of people danced and laughed only feet away from where she stood, locked in Eli's arms, concealed behind the column. The world faded away, narrowing to hold only Eli.

When at last he lifted his head, she was breathless. If she hadn't been supported against his solid strength, she knew she would have wobbled, her knees weak.

Eli's hooded gaze searched hers, his breath coming too fast. His fingertips moved reflexively against the bare skin of her back above the low-cut gown as if unable to keep from stroking, and a muscle ticked along the line of his jaw. Whatever he saw in her eyes had his lips curving upward in a slow, sensual half smile that made Frankie yearn for the feel of his mouth on hers again. Then he wrapped her closer and swept her out from behind the column, back into the crowd, the music a slow swirl of sound around them. Frankie let him guide her, her feet automatically moving to the rhythm as she struggled to clear her head.

She was every bit as shaken now as she'd been by that first kiss all those months ago at her birthday party. No question about it, she thought with faint dismay, when she'd felt the earth move during that first kiss, it hadn't been the result of drinking too much champagne on an empty stomach.

Because it had just happened again.

Harry and Cornelia, with half the dance floor now separating them from Eli and Frankie, were each trying to digest and interpret what they'd just seen.

"I haven't purposely spied on any of my daughters since they were teenagers," Cornelia told Harry. "I feel guilty."

"We didn't spy on them on purpose," Harry protested. "We just happened to be dancing near them when he pulled her behind that column. It's not as if we were using binoculars."

Cornelia leaned back against his arm and looked up at him. "Even you can't believe that excuse, Harry," she admonished him, shaking her head. "You know very well you asked me to dance solely to keep an eye on Frankie and Eli."

"All right," he admitted. "It's true. But in my defense, I'm having a hard time believing she's suddenly interested in Eli. They've known each other for years, and I've never seen a hint of anything romantic between them."

"Maybe that's precisely why," Cornelia pointed out. "Sometimes two people can be too close and not realize they're perfect for each other."

"I find that hard to believe," Harry scoffed, dismissing the concept. "If a man and a woman are thrown together often enough, sooner or later they'll realize they're attracted. Probably happen sooner rather than later," he added.

"Perhaps," Cornelia conceded. "But some people are *so* obtuse, they wouldn't see the perfect partner if they tripped over them."

Her voice held an underlying snap, but Harry didn't notice.

"Well, I still think Nicholas would make the perfect man for Frankie."

Cornelia's eyes widened, then narrowed over Harry's face. "Please tell me you're not matchmaking again, Harry."

Her voice held an ominous tone. Harry winced. "Now, Cornelia," he said persuasively, "what makes you think I'd do that?"

Cornelia wasn't entirely convinced but let the subject drop as the orchestra left the bandstand for a break and they returned to their table.

Three hours later, after dinner followed by more champagne and dancing, Eli handed Frankie into the back of the limousine once more.

The car moved smoothly away from the hotel portico. Outside the tinted windows, the glow of downtown Seattle's neon signs, bright car headlights and red taillights blurred into rivers of moving color in the rain.

Frankie sighed and relaxed, turning her head against the buttery soft leather seat to look at Eli. "I think we were a success tonight. Harry was clearly surprised to see you with me, although I'm not sure he's convinced yet that we're a couple. What do you think?"

"I suspect it's going to take more than one appearance to make Harry believe we're involved. He needs to be convinced you're crazy about me and unlikely to be interested in someone else if he's going to stop trying to hook you up with Nicholas." Eli's half smile was wry. "Harry's like a dog with a bone. Once he gets an idea in his head, it takes major evidence to get him to change his mind. He's stubborn."

"Then we'll just have to be even more determined—and outlast him. Are you up for that?"

Eli shrugged, his eyes glinting at the challenge. "I told you when we first talked about this that I didn't expect Harry to be easily convinced." He shrugged. "Tonight was just the opening salvo in a campaign—but in the end, we'll win."

Frankie stared at him, arrested. "You sound like a character out of the *Godfather* movies. I suppose next you'll be telling me we need to go to the mattresses."

He laughed out loud. "We might reach that point, knowing Harry."

"I know," Frankie murmured, distracted by the flash of his smile in the shadowy interior of the limo. "I confess, when I came up with this plan, I thought we could be seen together a couple of times and Harry would abandon his matchmaking schemes. I should have known he wouldn't give up so easily."

"Not to worry." Eli picked up her hand, threading her fingers through his before resting their joined hands on his thigh. "We're partners, right? The two of us together are a match for Harry."

The car slowed, pulling to the curb and stopping. Eli glanced out the window. "We're home." Before their driver could exit to open their door, Eli stepped out and opened an umbrella as he turned to lend Frankie a hand.

Rain pattered on the umbrella, but beneath it Frankie was warm and dry, tucked into the curve of Eli's side, his hand at her waist. They hurried up the sidewalk to the shelter of the condo building's wide overhang. The lobby was empty and quiet when they entered, the elevator and third-floor hallway equally hushed.

Frankie unlocked her door and turned, her shoulder brushing against Eli's black tux jacket. "I'll call you as soon as I talk to Mom and find out where we might run into Harry again," she told him.

"Sounds good." He leaned in and brushed a kiss against her mouth. "Good night," he murmured, his blue eyes darkened between half-lowered lashes.

"Good night," Frankie managed to respond before slipping inside and closing the door. She leaned back against the panels, hearing the sound of the elevator's ping announcing its arrival, then silence. She hurried across her living room and peered out through the blinds at the street below. Short moments later, Eli moved across the sidewalk and ducked into the waiting limo. Then the car pulled away from the curb and disappeared around the corner at the end of her street.

She left the window and moved slowly into her

bedroom, stripping off her coat and hanging it away in the closet before unzipping her gown and stepping out of it.

She couldn't stop thinking about Eli as she finished undressing, removing her bracelet. To her relief, the necklace clasp opened easily, and she tucked it and the bracelet into her jewelry box. But when she took off the matching earrings, she discovered one of them was missing. Despite searching the carpet and shaking out the green gown and evening coat, she didn't find the one-of-a-kind heirloom. With sinking heart, she added the single earring to the lacquered jewelry box and closed the lid.

I can't imagine how I'll find a jeweler to create a matching earring, she thought as she slipped into pink flannel pajama bottoms and a cotton tank top.

The troubling loss of her earring was soon set aside as she returned to thoughts of Eli. So far, her plan to erase unrealistic romantic notions left over from her teenage years was failing miserably. Eli Wolf was even more charming than she'd expected.

And kissing him could prove to be addictive, she thought as she settled under the comforter and turned out the lamp.

She still believed her plan to make Harry cease his matchmaking by convincing him she was madly in love with Eli would work.

But she wasn't nearly as positive that spending more time with Eli would cure her of her high school crush. In fact, she suspected it just might do the opposite.

Chapter Five

On Sunday afternoon following the fundraiser for the Children's Hospital, Frankie drove to her mother's house. She was sure Cornelia would question her about Eli, but her mother didn't raise the subject as they chatted about the success of the event while brewing a pot of tea in the kitchen. While Frankie loaded a tray with the Wedgwood teapot and cups, Cornelia carried napkins and a plate of shortbread biscuits out to the front porch just as a white pickup with a Wolf Construction logo on the doors pulled to a stop at the curb.

"Frankie," Cornelia called, peering out a tall window as the driver stepped out of the pickup. "Isn't that Eli? Were you expecting him?"

Frankie stepped out onto the porch, carrying the tea

tray. She set the heavy silver tray on the low table in front of her mother and looked out the window.

There was no mistaking the tall, broad-shouldered man strolling up the walk—and no denying the swift surge of pleased surprise the sight of him elicited in Frankie.

"It *is* Eli—but I have no idea why he's here."

Cornelia had renovated the porch of her beautifully restored Queen Anne home and enclosed the wide space with waist-high windows. Now it was an extension of the living room, a wide glassed-in entry room that ran the length of the front of the house. Lazily turning wooden fans were suspended from the high ceiling; the floor was painted a glossy gray, and area rugs dotted the gleaming wood boards. Chairs and sofas of white wicker with colorful pillows were grouped in comfortable seating areas down the length of the room. At the moment, Cornelia sat in an armchair, its soft cushions covered in bright cotton with a coral and green floral pattern. Frankie took a seat on the padded white wooden swing, within reach of the low wicker table where she'd set the tea tray.

Eli glanced up as he neared, his gaze meeting Frankie's through the glass. He smiled, his stride quickening as he loped up the three shallow steps to the door.

"Come in, Eli," Cornelia called.

"Hello, ladies."

Frankie felt the room shrink as he stepped inside and closed the door, his presence seeming to suck up the oxygen. He wore faded jeans, black boots, and a pale blue polo shirt under a worn brown bomber jacket. Raindrops glistened in his black hair as he shrugged out of his jacket and hung the damp leather over the back of a nearby rocking chair.

She drew a deep breath and patted the cushion beside her. "I didn't expect to see you today—how did you know I was here?"

"I stopped by Justin and Lily's place to deliver the plans for Ava's rabbit hutch—which has turned into a rabbit-condo-castle," he said with a wry grin. "Lily told me you'd mentioned spending the afternoon with your mom, so I thought I'd drop by on my way home." He shoved one hand into his jeans pocket and pulled out a glittering jet and gold earring. "You lost this in the car last night. I thought you might be worried about it."

"Oh, you found it! Thank goodness." Frankie held out her cupped hand, and Eli dropped the earring into her palm.

He settled onto the swing, one arm stretched out along the seat back behind her.

"I was so upset—I was afraid I'd lost it forever." Impulsively, she leaned sideways into Eli and kissed his cheek. "Thank you!"

"You're welcome." His eyes smiled at her. "Feel free to lose jewelry in my car anytime. I like the way you say thank you."

Frankie felt heat move up her cheeks and knew her face was no doubt pink. She shot a quick glance at her mother from beneath lowered lashes. An amused, indulgent smile played about Cornelia's lips. Apparently, her mother approved of Eli's charm.

"I hope I don't lose track of any more family heirlooms in the future, but if I do, it's nice to know you'll find them for me." She patted his cheek with easy familiarity and shifted back, away from the hard curve of his body. Pretending she didn't miss the sheer pleasure she felt in leaning against his warm strength, she leaned forward and picked up the Wedgwood teapot. "Mom and I are having Earl Grey—would you like a cup?"

She poured and handed Cornelia a delicate cup and saucer before glancing inquiringly at Eli.

"Tea?" He winced. "Honey, you know I don't do tea."

She couldn't help laughing at his apologetic but pained expression. "I'm sure Mom has something else to drink."

"Actually, I just had hot chocolate with Ava, so I'm good."

"Did you drink it out of a mug or a thimble-sized toy china teacup?" Frankie asked, stirring sugar into her own tea before sitting back on the swing, cup in hand, one foot tucked beneath her so she could face Eli.

"Today we sat at the kitchen-island counter and had normal size mugs," Eli told her. He shook his head. "Thank God. I can hardly pick up those tiny cups of hers. Not to mention, sitting at that little-girl table scares me. I'm constantly worrying the chair won't hold me and I'll break it."

Frankie and Cornelia smiled with sympathy. Frankie

had a swift mental image of Eli's tall, broad body perched on one of Ava's child-sized chairs. The picture was endearing.

"Do you see a lot of Ava?" she asked, sipping her tea.

"Not as much as I'd like—Justin has to spend quite a bit of time on his ranch in Idaho." He leaned forward, taking a shortbread biscuit from the plate on the tea tray. "But when they're in Seattle, we get together fairly often." He glanced at Frankie, the tiny smile lines at the corners of his eyes crinkling. "I'm her honorary uncle, and apparently Ava thinks that requires certain duties."

"One of which is having tea with her dolls?" Frankie guessed.

"Yeah, that's one of them." He pretended to shudder, but the fond smile barely curving his lips told her he didn't really mind playing tea party with the little girl.

Rain pattered against the glass. Frankie sighed and eyed the wet world outside with gloom. "I think I'll cancel tonight. The thought of standing around in the rain at a campus rally for world peace doesn't appeal."

Eli gave her disbelieving look. "You were going to join a bunch of college kids, in the rain, to listen to a freshman lecture everyone about solving the world's ills?"

"How did you know the scheduled speaker is a freshman?" she asked, intrigued.

He shrugged. "They're always freshmen—by their second year in college, students are more cynical." He lowered his voice. "Rumor has it, the change is due to the amount of beer consumed at all those freshman frat parties."

Cornelia laughed. "I think you may be right, Eli."

"He could be." Frankie tried to hold back a smile but failed. "I bet you formed this opinion through first-hand experience," she said dryly.

"I have to confess I helped lower the beer level in a few kegs during my freshman year at college," he confirmed. "But I never picked up a bullhorn and lectured the student population on a solution for world peace."

"Did you rally for any good causes?" Cornelia asked him.

Curled next to him on the cushioned wooden bench seat, Frankie sipped her tea and listened as Eli bantered back and forth with her mother about his activities in college. He'd been a part of their extended group of family friends for a long time through his friendship with Justin. She knew he'd attended the University of Washington by combining scholarships and working at Wolf Construction. By the time he'd earned an engineering degree, Wolf Construction's business had taken off under his leadership and become a major contender for commercial building in Seattle and the surrounding area.

Everything Harry had told her about Nicholas Dean's success could be said of Eli, she thought, feeling a surge of pride at his accomplishments.

Eli glanced sideways at her, his gaze warming.

"Come to the movies with me tonight, Frankie," he

said easily. "We'll be inside a theater, we'll be dry and I'll buy you buttered popcorn."

"What movie are you going to see?" she asked, aware of her mother listening.

"An action adventure based on a book by one of my favorite authors."

"Sounds like fun."

He eyed her. "You like those kinds of books, too?"

"Why wouldn't I?"

His blue eyes gleamed with approval. "I'll be damned. I keep learning things about you that amaze me."

Frankie huffed. "Lots of women read suspense novels."

"I know, but you have a PhD in English literature. Somehow, I didn't expect you to like action-adventure fiction."

"I'd be just as interested if there was a new film based on one of Jane Austen's titles," Frankie said firmly. "But I'm not a snob about books—I like all different kinds. I'd love to see the movie tonight."

"Great." Eli looked at Cornelia. "How about you, Cornelia? Would you like to come with us?"

"Oh, no." Cornelia waved a hand. "My favorite mystery series is on PBS tonight, and I've been looking forward to the next installment. I'm going to curl up in my jammies in front of the TV with a bowl of ice cream."

"All right, but you know you're welcome to join us if you change your mind," Eli told her. He looked at Frankie. "I'll pick you up at seven?"

She nodded. "I'll be ready. What theater are we going to?"

"Pacific Place downtown." He stood, the swing dipping and swaying on the heavy chains suspending the seat. "I'd better get going. I need to run by a construction site and check with the security guard."

"Is there a problem?" Frankie felt a swift stab of concern.

"Only with water—we've had a lot of rain the last couple of days. I want to make sure there's no flooding." He took his jacket from the back of the chair and shrugged into it.

Cornelia rose, collecting the tea tray. "It was lovely to see you, Eli—stop by again soon."

"I will, Cornelia, thank you."

Her slim figure disappeared into the front hall.

Eli held out his hand, and Frankie put her fingers in his, letting him pull her to her feet. He slung an arm over her shoulders, tucking her against his side, and walked her toward the outside door.

"I hope you don't mind my dropping by without calling. But when Justin told me you were spending the afternoon with your mom, I thought it was a perfect opportunity to return your earring and spend a little time reinforcing Cornelia's belief that we're a couple."

"I don't mind at all—I'm glad you stopped by. I confess I don't like keeping the truth from Mom. The only thing that makes me feel okay about deceiving her is that I know she'd be the first to join us if she knew Harry was meddling again."

"I suspect you're right about Cornelia. But the more people who know about our plan, the more difficult it would be to keep it a secret from Harry, I'm afraid."

Frankie sighed. "I'm sure you're right."

He stopped at the door, turning to face her, his back to the screen and glass and the gray rain outside.

"You don't have to take me to the movie tonight, Eli. Mom will never know."

He lifted an eyebrow. "Are you kidding? Hanging out with you is one of the perks of this scam. Besides, it's always more fun to watch a movie with someone. Then later you can go over the good parts, or, if it's a bad film, you can commiserate and complain about all the lousy acting and special effects."

"Ah, I see. So it's not that you want my company," she teased, inordinately pleased that she'd see him later, "it's that you want someone to compare opinions with after the credits roll."

He laughed. "You've caught me, that's part of it." He bent his head to whisper in her ear. "Your mom is standing at the kitchen sink. If she looks sideways, she can see us. Want to give her something to tell Harry?"

"Okay." Frankie nodded, her heartbeat beginning to race as his mouth curved in a slow smile at her assent.

He slipped his arms around her waist and eased her nearer, lifting her up on her toes as his head bent.

Warm, seductive, his mouth coaxed hers to respond. Frankie clutched his biceps, her head spinning as the world narrowed to the hard body she leaned against and Eli's lips on hers.

The kiss only lasted a moment. Too soon, Eli lifted his head, easing her back off her toes.

"I'll pick you up at seven," he murmured, blue eyes darkened to navy.

She nodded, unable to gather her wits and form a sentence.

He bent, his lips brushing against the sensitive shell of her ear. "And, Frankie, kissing you is one of the best parts of this scheme."

Frankie felt her eyes widen. Then he shoved the door open behind him and, with a quick grin, left her. The door closed on his back as he loped down the sidewalk. Moments later, his pickup truck accelerated away from the curb.

He's right, she thought, still faintly dazed. *Kissing is definitely one of the perks of having Eli pretend to be my boyfriend.*

Eli arrived at Frankie's condo that evening and within a short half hour, they'd reached the Pacific Place and were settled into comfortable seats in a row near the back of the theater. He held her coat while she slipped out of it before handing her the container of popcorn.

"This is a lot of popcorn for only two people," she said, eyeing the bucket dubiously.

"I like popcorn. Trust me." He winked at her. "It won't last long."

Frankie laughed and took a handful of the salty kernels. As she ate, she glanced around the theater. The lights were still on and local business advertisements played with minimal sound on the wide screen up front.

"This reminds me of going to the movies with Mom and my sisters when we were little," she said. "I love rainy Sundays at the theater."

"Granddad used to drop off me and my brothers at the theater in Ballard on Saturday or Sunday afternoons," Eli told her. "I suspect it gave him a much-needed break."

"I'm sure Mom enjoyed the peace and quiet when we all were focused on the screen, too," Frankie replied. "Parenting looks like a tough job when there are two people, but being a single parent must be beyond difficult."

"I agree." Eli nodded. "Watching Justin and Lily with Ava has been a real eye-opener. Don't get me wrong," he added hastily. "I think she's great, but, man, she wears me out."

"I know what you mean. Ava has nonstop energy." Frankie smiled with affection as she sipped her water. "I have a play date scheduled with her on Saturday morning and I'm wondering if I should increase my vitamin intake and start lifting weights to build my endurance."

Eli grinned at her. "Might not be a bad idea. Aren't you a little old to have play dates?"

"Absolutely not," Frankie said emphatically. "I adore Ava and every third Saturday, we get together to go to the park or the zoo or a children's exhibition at the Seattle Center. Of course," she added with a twinkle,

"I call it bonding, but Ava insists we're having play dates."

"Ah." Eli nodded. "Makes sense. So what else did you do when you were a child?" Eli asked. "Besides go to movies on Sunday afternoons."

"Skipped rope, rode bikes, played Monopoly with my sisters, and—" Frankie paused to sip her water "—volunteered at a horse rescue barn in Arlington."

Arrested, Eli stopped eating popcorn, one eyebrow rising in query. "I didn't know you were interested in horses. I thought you were a city girl, through and through."

"I suppose I am to a certain extent," Frankie agreed. "But I love animals, especially horses. When I celebrated my eighth birthday, Mom told me it was time for me to pick a cause to donate my time to and I chose abused horses."

"Good choice." Eli nodded, his eyes gleaming with approval. "When Granddad told us we were old enough to start giving back to the community, I picked Habitat for Humanity."

"That's a wonderful cause," Frankie enthused. "I've considered signing up, but I don't know anything about carpentry."

"A lot of volunteers don't when they start. Join my group," he said. "I'll make sure you learn how to swing a hammer and saw a board."

"I doubt it's that easy," she said with a shake of her head.

He shrugged. "It's not complicated—and professional

carpenters team with new volunteers to supervise them."

"If you promise to teach me enough about carpentry so my contribution doesn't result in a house falling down, I'll sign up," she told him.

He laughed. "You couldn't make a house fall down. Don't worry about it."

Before Frankie could respond, the house lights dimmed and the previews for upcoming movies began.

When the popcorn container was empty and napkins had wiped away any traces of salt and butter, Eli caught her hand in his, threading her fingers between his own. Startled, she glanced sideways at him, but he was focused on the screen, his profile lit by the flickering light from the movie.

There was something nice about sitting in the dark theater, Eli's warm, callused palm pressed to hers, the hard strength of his shoulder against hers.

Frankie turned back toward the screen, deciding to enjoy the moment and not worry about what it might mean that her heart stuttered each time his thumb smoothed over the back of her hand.

Since they both had to rise early for work the following morning, Eli dropped her off just after ten-thirty, saying good-night with another kiss that left her breathless. Forty minutes later, as she climbed into bed and switched off the lamp, Frankie realized she hadn't spent such a relaxing, thoroughly enjoyable evening in a very long time.

And it was entirely due to Eli's company.

Part of her loved the thought—while another part dealt with the niggling worry that she liked his company far too much.

A wise woman wouldn't tempt fate, she thought drowsily.

Chapter Six

On Wednesday morning, Frankie was in her office at Liberty Hall on the University of Washington campus. Since completing work on a museum exhibit in December, she'd been reassigned from her usual duties as a research assistant. She was now temporarily filling in for an English Literature professor who'd gone on emergency leave. Much as she loved the variety of her research work, Frankie welcomed the opportunity to teach in a classroom. The new responsibility challenged her creativity and gave her one-on-one contact with students, which wasn't usually the case.

Since her next lecture wasn't for another forty-five minutes, she planned to make good use of the time to catch up on a few non-classroom duties.

Her desk was littered with data reports, printouts of

class grading curves and miscellaneous information. Deep in thought, she contemplated a possible change in her syllabus notes for the current lecture series on classic British authors of the twentieth century.

"Hey, Professor." The deep male voice was soft, just above a murmur, but Frankie jumped nonetheless, startled, her gaze flying to the doorway.

Eli leaned against the doorjamb, one broad shoulder propped against the walnut edge. He was dressed for work in a blue-and-white plaid flannel shirt that hung unbuttoned over a white T-shirt tucked into the waistband of snug faded jeans. A black leather belt was threaded through the belt loops of the jeans, and dusty black boots covered his feet.

"Hey," she responded faintly.

"Sorry I startled you." He shoved away from the doorjamb and walked toward her, his stride easy. "I had to stop at a job site near here, and when I picked up coffee, I thought about you, probably stuck in your office, slaving away. So I brought you a latte—double shot, vanilla, right?" He held up two take-out Starbucks cups with lids.

Frankie beamed at him, delighted. "You remembered." She took the cup and sipped, closing her eyes in pleasure. "I owe you."

"And I'll collect," he shot back, grinning when her eyes opened and she studied him with suspicion. He picked up a straightback wooden chair and spun it around, straddling it, his forearms resting along the top of the polished oak back. "Any new thoughts about our next move against Harry?"

Frankie leaned back in her swivel chair, propping her stockinged feet atop the open bottom desk drawer, ankles crossed. "Believe it or not, Harry called this morning. He's having a group of people over for dinner on Friday night to welcome a visiting software mogul from London. He asked if I'd like to join them." She looked at Eli from beneath lowered lashes. "I told him yes, providing I could bring a date."

"And what did Harry say?" Eli drawled, lifting his cup to sip, his blue eyes watching her over the rim.

"He asked me if my date was Nicholas Dean."

Eli stiffened, his eyes narrowing over her. "He's still pushing Dean at you."

Frankie nodded. "Apparently."

"Has Dean called you?" Eli asked, his voice neutral.

"Interestingly enough, no, he hasn't." Frankie tucked her hair behind her ear.

Eli's gaze tracked her fingers' movement, lingering over her hair before fastening on her face once again. "So Harry must not be giving Dean the same kind of verbal nudging he's giving you," he guessed.

"I suspect not." Frankie frowned, considering. "Has Harry tried to grill you about me?"

"Not yet." Eli shrugged. "But we have a meeting tomorrow to discuss the Wolf Construction proposal for the south Seattle project. Maybe he's waiting until then." He sipped his coffee once again. "Harry's cagey—I wouldn't put anything past him, and if he's not nudging Nicholas about asking you out, he must have a reason."

"Or maybe Nicholas refused to get involved in Harry's schemes," Frankie said. "And if he did, then our plan isn't really necessary."

Eli's eyes glinted. "If you believe that, then you don't know Harry as well as I thought you did."

"What makes you say that?" Frankie hoped Eli had a really good answer, because she was enjoying seeing him and didn't want their dates to end.

"Harry always has a bigger view of his projects, and if fixing you up with Nicholas didn't work out, he would go to plan B."

"And what's plan B?" Frankie asked.

"Not what—*who*. I have no idea who Harry would pick out to be the next candidate, but I'm sure he has another name on his list as a backup for Nicholas."

"Of course." Frankie sighed, tense muscles relaxing. "You're right. Harry always has a plan. Mom said that's the reason he was always so good at chess."

"That sounds like Harry." Eli glanced at his watch. "Time for me to go—I have an appointment in fifteen minutes." He stood, swinging the chair back into its original position. "What time do you want me to pick you up on Friday?"

"How about seven?"

"I'll see you then." His gaze flicked to her mouth, lingered, before returning to her eyes. "Have a good afternoon," he murmured, his deep voice a rumble.

And he was gone, before Frankie could gather her wits after that hot, focused stare.

Several minutes later, she was still sitting motionless, staring blankly at the notes on her desk when, for the second time in a half hour, knuckles rapped against her open office door. She looked up to find her friend and coworker, assistant professor Sharon Katz, standing on the threshold. Before Frankie could say hello, Sharon spoke.

"Wow, Frankie, who was that guy?" she asked, curiosity lighting her face. "He's gorgeous."

Frankie laughed at her friend's expression. "He's a friend of my cousin Justin."

"And he's visiting you…why?"

"He brought me a latte." Frankie lifted the Starbucks cup and saluted Sharon with it before drinking.

"Nice." Sharon leaned against the doorjamb, arms crossed, a sheaf of papers in one hand. "Come on, fess up. Are you dating him?"

"I am." Frankie grinned when Sharon rolled her eyes and fanned herself with the papers.

"Way to go, Professor." She straightened, glancing over her shoulder. "Darn, students are already filing into my lecture hall. I have to go—let's have lunch tomorrow, and you can fill me in on all the details, okay?"

"Okay." Frankie turned back to the half-completed report on her desk as Sharon disappeared, the quick tap of her heels fading away down the hall.

Anticipation buoyed Frankie over the next day. But Friday morning brought disappointing news. Her department head emailed to tell her attendance was mandatory at an impromptu after-work cocktail party. She suspected her boss wanted to impress his superiors with the presence of the entire department.

Disappointed that she had to cancel her plans with Eli that evening, Frankie dialed his cell phone several times, but each time the call went immediately to his answering service. As the morning flew by and became afternoon, she grew more concerned that she wouldn't be able to catch him before he left the house to pick her up at her condo.

She tried reaching him at the office, but when the message center picked up, she remembered Eli telling her that he'd given the secretaries the afternoon off. She left a message with the answering service but the operator couldn't guarantee Eli would get it before Monday morning when the office staff returned and picked up messages.

Frankie hated the thought that Eli might think she'd stood him up but couldn't think of another way to reach him.

Unless she could catch him on a job site, she thought with sudden inspiration.

She collected her purse and left her office in Liberty Hall. She was fairly certain she knew the address of the Wolf Construction site not far from campus. She had no idea whether Eli would be there or not, but she hoped to find someone who could tell her how to contact him. Within ten minutes, after a wrong turn that had her backing out of a dead-end street, she found the site.

The skeleton of what would become an upscale, five-story condo building rose in the air above her as she turned off the street and onto the bumpy dirt lot. Puddles of water left by the early morning downpour dotted the ground, and Frankie avoided them as best she could. Still, she knew her just-washed BMW would need another bath, and soon.

A contractor's trailer stood at the end of the lot, and several pickup trucks were parked in front of it, two of which had Wolf Construction logos on their doors. Frankie hoped that meant Eli was in the trailer, and she mentally crossed her fingers as she parked next to one of the trucks and got out.

Skirting a muddy puddle, she climbed the two wooden steps and knocked on the metal trailer door.

"Come in."

Frankie didn't recognize the deep male voice, but nevertheless she pushed the door open and stepped inside, halting abruptly.

Three men stood at a drafting table that was littered with blueprints and notes. A fourth man, his eyes bright blue in a lined face below a shock of white hair, sat in a battered office chair, one foot propped on the opposite knee as he leaned back.

None of the four were Eli. All of them were big, broad and dressed alike in faded jeans, plaid flannel shirts and muddy work boots. And all of them watched her with alert male gazes.

Frankie returned their interested stares with a friendly but reserved glance. She'd never met Eli's brothers or his grandfather, but the resemblance was unmistakable. These four had to be related to him.

"Hello. I'm looking for Eli Wolf."

"I'm his brother Connor," one of three men at the table drawled. "You're too pretty for Eli, honey. I'd be happy to help you—with whatever you need."

Taken aback, Frankie was speechless for only a second before the twinkle in Connor's eye reassured her. She smiled. "Sorry—honey—but it's Eli I need to find."

"Smart woman."

The deep, amused voice came from her left, and before Frankie could fully turn, Eli slipped an arm around her waist and bent to brush a quick kiss against her cheek.

"Hi, Frankie. What are you doing here?"

"I've been trying to reach you, but you didn't answer your cell phone," she told him. "I have to go to a faculty cocktail party right after work, so I can't make dinner at Harry's tonight. I'm sorry to cancel so late, but my boss just informed me attendance is mandatory. Apparently, the department head wants to impress the university president with our show of support." She grimaced. "I'd rather spend an hour or two being tortured by cannibals, but I can't get out of it."

"Sounds pretty bad," he said with sympathy. "Did you let your mom know we won't be able to join her at Harry's?"

She nodded. "Mom said she'd apologize to Harry for me." She looked up at him. "You should go, anyway—

everyone has to eat, right? And maybe you could pin Harry down about the contract."

He shook his head. "No, thanks—I think I'll pass." He smiled, a slow curve of his lips that made her breath hitch. "Just wouldn't be the same without you."

"I hate to interrupt you two," Connor broke in. "But don't you think you should introduce us to the lady, Eli?"

Frankie had been so focused on Eli that she'd all but forgotten the presence of the other four men. Now she realized they were all watching her and Eli with interest and curiosity. Even the older man had a curious gleam in his eye.

"Sorry," Eli said easily, clearly not the slightest bit concerned at Connor's inference he'd been lacking in manners. "Frankie Fairchild, these are my brothers— Connor, Ethan and Matthew. And the gentleman in the chair there is our grandfather, Jack." He bent to whisper in her ear, loud enough that the others could hear. "All of them are disreputable and untrustworthy, and they cheat at cards—so watch out if you ever get in a poker game with them."

"Good afternoon," Frankie said, her amused gaze meeting each of theirs. Eli's three brothers were as tall, brawny and as handsome—each in his own way—as Eli. They all had coal-black hair and blue eyes and an air of assured male strength. In fact, she thought dazedly, the amount of testosterone filling the air was palpable. She glanced at Jack and found him watching her shrewdly. She felt her cheeks warm under his knowing gaze.

"They're kind of overwhelming, all in one room, aren't they, missy?" he asked, his blue eyes warming. "Just like their grandpa, they have to beat women off with a stick."

"Geez, Granddad," Matt groaned, giving Frankie an apologetic look. "Sorry, Frankie. We can dress him up but can't take him out—not anywhere in polite company, at least."

"Hmmph," the older man snorted. "Who'd have guessed I'd run into polite company in a construction trailer? Usually it's just you four, and you don't qualify as polite."

Frankie laughed out loud. She could easily see the affection between the four brothers and their grandfather and was charmed. "I'd better get going." Frankie looked up at Eli and found him watching her, his blue eyes half concealed by thick lashes as he looked down at her. "I'm keeping you from your work, and I have a class in—" she glanced at her wristwatch "—twenty-five minutes. I'll leave and let you all get back to what you were doing." She waved a hand at the drafting table with its unrolled stack of blueprints held flat by a large rock sitting on each corner.

"You're not keeping us from work," Eli told her.

"Not at all," Ethan added, his voice a slow, deep drawl.

"We were all tired of looking at these damn blueprints," Connor added.

"Nevertheless, I'd better get back to campus." Frankie turned, and Eli was there before her, opening the door and holding it for her. "It was nice to meet you," she told the four Wolf men.

They echoed a chorus of goodbyes, and Frankie stepped outside, followed by Eli, who pulled the door shut.

"Where are you parked?" He frowned at the wet ground.

"Just over there." Frankie pointed at her car, just beyond the big dual-wheeled white pickup.

Eli took her elbow, scanning the ground between the steps and her car before walking beside her. "You're not wearing the right kind of boots for this weather. I'll get you a pair of rubber mud boots to keep in your car."

Frankie felt inordinately pleased that he seemed to expect her to visit again. "That would be nice," she murmured.

They reached her BMW, and he pulled open the door.

"How long do you think you'll have to stay at the cocktail party tonight?" he asked, leaning on the open door to look down at her as she turned the ignition key.

"Not too long, I hope," she told him. "I'm planning to slip out as soon as possible and head home. It's been a long week—I think I'll curl up in front of the TV and watch something mindless."

He chuckled. "Sounds like a good plan. Drive carefully." He stood back, closing the door with a quiet thunk.

As Frankie negotiated the bumps and puddles of the

lot and turned onto the smoothly paved street, she could see Eli in the rearview mirror. He stood, hands thrust in jeans pockets, the sun glinting off his black hair, watching her drive away.

She'd been looking forward to seeing him this evening, and having to cancel their dinner date made the prospect of the boring cocktail party seem even more dull.

She turned a corner and could no longer see Eli nor the construction site.

No doubt about it, she thought with a sigh. She was much more interested in spending an evening with Eli than schmoozing at a cocktail party with her boss and coworkers.

Apparently, she wasn't immune to the lure of a tall, dark and handsome man. Especially not when the man was Eli.

Eli watched Frankie's car disappear into traffic before he turned and reentered the work trailer.

"Pretty woman, Eli. Where'd you meet her?" Connor asked.

"Does she have a sister?" Matt asked, grinning when Eli shot him a quick glare as he crossed to the kitchenette and poured a mug of coffee.

"Yes, she has sisters, and no, I'm not going to introduce you," Eli said as Matt's eyes lit with interest. "And I've known her since she was just a kid."

"Yeah?" Ethan frowned at him. "I don't remember a girl named Frankie."

"Francesca Fairchild—she's Justin's cousin."

"I still don't remember her," Connor said.

"She must be Cornelia Fairchild's daughter," Jack said with a decisive nod. "Cornelia's the widow of Harry Hunt's original partner—I heard the families stayed close after Cornelia's husband died, and the girls consider Harry their uncle and his boys their cousins."

"That's right." Eli carried his mug to the drafting table and set it on the ledge above the blueprints. "Frankie's closer to Justin than any of his brothers. I met her through Justin when she was still in grade school."

"Was she gorgeous in grade school, too?" Matt asked.

"She's always been pretty," Eli answered shortly. He leveled a lethal glare at Matt. "And she's off-limits."

"Whoa." Matt took a step back, lifting his hands in mock defense, palms out. "Sorry, big brother. Didn't know you'd already staked a claim."

Ethan laughed, Jack's chuckle joining him.

"You must be blind, Matt," Connor said. "Nobody could have missed that whole she's-mine-touch-her-you-die thing Eli had going on a few minutes ago."

Matt's deep laugh joined the other three, and Eli threw them a disgusted glare.

"Can we move past this and get back to work?"

"Sure," Matt said, his eyes twinkling as he clapped Eli on the shoulder. "It's nice to see you getting irritated with us over a woman, Eli. Must mean you're finally recovered from the accident and back to normal."

Eli growled a noncommittal response, and the conversation returned to finding a solution for a glitch in the design of the second-floor balcony supports.

Later, when his brothers and Jack left the trailer and he was alone, Eli's thoughts returned to Frankie.

Where the hell had that surge of possessiveness come from when she'd stepped into the trailer and met his brothers? The Wolf men had hammered out an unwritten rule while in their teens—none of them ever poached each other's dates. He had no reason to worry that Matt, Ethan or Connor would do more than flirt harmlessly with Frankie as long as he was dating her.

He'd never before felt the urge to threaten his brothers over a woman. So, why now—and why Frankie?

"The protective thing must be left over from Justin and me vetting her boyfriends when she was a teenager," he muttered aloud, frowning unseeingly at the drawings taped on the wall.

Of course that was it, he thought with relief. He'd known Frankie a long time—it was only natural he'd feel protective. No doubt if he'd had a sister, he'd feel the same way.

A small voice in his head uttered a loud *hah!*

Eli ignored it, grabbed his hardhat and left the trailer to purposely stay busy so he wouldn't have time to ponder all the reasons why he might feel so strongly about Frankie and other men.

Even if the other men were his brothers.

Even if he knew she was perfectly safe with them.

It was going to be a long afternoon, he thought with resignation.

It was nearly seven o'clock before Frankie reached home that evening. The afternoon sunshine had given way to dark skies and sheets of rain that drenched her as she ran from her car. She shrugged out of her raincoat, hanging it on a hook beside the door, then toed off her wet pumps the moment she closed and locked the condo door behind her. Bending to pick them up, she walked in damp-stockinged feet into her bedroom. She dropped her purse and leather briefcase onto the bed, set her shoes next to the floor heat vent and stripped off her jacket, blouse, skirt and hose.

She flipped on lights as she went, turning on the shower and letting it run to heat up the space while she shed bra and panties, dropping them into the hamper before she stepped into the shower.

The water pulsed against her skin, and she turned her face into the spray, relishing its heat for several moments before she shampooed and scrubbed.

She felt a thousand times better when she left the bathroom. She'd towel-dried her hair then run a brush through the tangles until it lay sleek and smooth before donning a clean black bra, panties and gray University of Washington sweatpants. She drew on a matching gray UW hoodie, zipping the front closed to a few inches below her collarbones.

Her stomach growled as she walked barefoot into

the living room, pausing to switch on the television to a cable twenty-four-hour news channel before heading for the kitchen. She shifted items on the refrigerator shelves, but nothing appealed. She was just contemplating calling a local Chinese restaurant to order delivery when the doorbell rang.

Sighing, she padded out of the kitchen, across the living room to the tiny entryway. *I bet it's Mrs. Ankiewicz,* she thought. Her eighty-year-old neighbor often dropped in on a Friday evening if Frankie was home. Much as she adored the feisty old lady and enjoyed their conversations, however, she was more interested in food at the moment.

One glance through her front door's small glass viewer, however, had Frankie catching her breath.

Eli stood in the hall outside.

The sense of disappointment she'd felt since leaving him at the work site lifted, instantly replaced by a surge of delight.

Oh, no! Her fingers tightened on the doorknob. She leaned her forehead against the solid wood door panel, nearly groaning in disbelief.

What happened to her determination not to give in to her attraction to him? She knew he was dangerous for her heart—she did *not* want to take any of this too seriously.

She lifted her head, narrowing her eyes at her reflection in the mirror.

We're just two people conspiring to teach Uncle Harry a lesson, she told her reflection sternly. Eli isn't really interested in me—I'm not his girlfriend and he's not my boyfriend.

Not really. She repeated the words in her mind but she couldn't ignore the mirror's reflection of the anticipation that flushed her cheeks and sparkled in her eyes.

She turned away from the mirror and its too-revealing image, drawing a deep breath and straightening her lips in an attempt to erase the smile.

Then she pulled open the door.

Chapter Seven

"Hi." Unfortunately, she suspected her expression told him exactly how happy she was to see him, but she couldn't bring herself to care. "I wasn't expecting you tonight."

"I thought you might be hungry, so I picked up a pizza—unless the food at the party was good...?" He lifted a square box in one hand; his other held a six-pack of imported beer.

"The food was awful, actually. Come in." She caught his arm and pulled him inside, closing the door to lead him to the kitchen. "You're drenched. It must be raining harder than it was when I came home." She drew in a deep breath when he set the pizza box down on the table and lifted the top. "That smells like heaven." With perfect timing, her stomach let out a low rumble.

"I'm guessing that means you *are* hungry?" A smile curved his lips as he shrugged out of his damp jacket and hung it over the back of a chair. He wore faded, well-worn jeans and a light blue polo shirt, the fabric stretching snugly over the hard, defined muscles of chest and thighs.

"That means I'm starving!" She laughed and opened cabinet doors to take out plates. "Why don't you take off your boots and set them on the floor grate over there." She pointed at the scrollwork vent under the window. "I use the vents for my shoes all the time—works like a charm."

Eli nodded and pulled off his boots, padding in stockinged feet to set them on the grate.

"Will you grab some napkins out of the drawer next to the sink?" Frankie plied a wheeled cutter with quick efficiency, cutting the pizza into slices.

They carried loaded plates and napkins into the living room, Eli balancing two bottles of beer and a single glass for Frankie.

"Are you sure you don't want a glass?" she asked, curling one leg beneath her as she sat on the sofa, balancing her plate on her lap.

"Positive." Eli set his plate on the coffee table while he removed bottle caps, pouring a glass for Frankie and setting it on the lamp table next to her at the end of the sofa. "Real men drink beer straight from the bottle."

Frankie rolled her eyes at him. "I'll let that pass," she said magnanimously. "I'm feeling kindly toward you

since you knocked on my door bearing edible gifts."
She lifted her slice of pizza. "Mmm."

Moments passed while they concentrated on their
pizza.

"So, how boring was the cocktail party?" Eli asked
after he'd finished his first slice.

"Deadly."

"That bad, huh?"

Frankie pursed her lips, considering. "On the scale
of really bad, it was somewhere between the torture of
sitting through an hour lecture on the conception process
of boll weevils and the Spanish Inquisition."

"Whoa." He held up his hands in surrender. "I'm not
even going to tell you about the most boring work party
I was ever forced to attend. You win."

She smiled sunnily, the last remnants of weary annoyance from a long day fading away. "Sometimes parties
at work aren't boring—I think this one wasn't enjoyable
because it was last-minute on a Friday night. Plus I was
annoyed that it forced me to change our plans."

"I know what you mean." He nodded and picked
up another pizza slice. They ate in companionable
silence.

Frankie finished her second piece with a sigh of con-
tentment, set her plate on the coffee table and picked up
the remote.

"Is there anything you want to watch?"

"ESPN."

"No."

"Oh, come on," he coaxed. "I brought you pizza—and there's a Knicks game on tonight."

"How about a compromise? I won't make you watch a chick flick if you don't make me watch a ball game."

He tipped his bottle and eyed her over the rim. "How about a guy movie?"

She narrowed her eyes suspiciously. "What, exactly, are we talking about here?"

"Cruise through the channel listings and I'll show you."

"Okay." Frankie thumbed the remote and brought up the channel log. "See anything interesting?"

They finally settled on an action film starring Will Smith.

As the opening credits began to roll, rain hammered against the windows outside. January in Seattle often brought winter storms roaring in off the Pacific to pound the city with wind and rain. Tonight was clearly no exception.

Inside, Frankie curled her legs under her. Eli stretched his long legs out in front of him, propping his feet on the coffee table, ankles crossed.

The wind whistled around the corner of the building. Frankie looked at the windows, where the shadowy shapes of tree branches, tossing in the wind, were visible in the faint glow from streetlights.

"Brr." She shivered, clutching a throw pillow against her middle. "I'm glad we're not at Harry's. We'd have to drive home in this."

"It's nasty out there," Eli agreed. He looked sideways

at her. "Come here." He reached out and wrapped one arm around her shoulders, toppling her sideways against him. Her head rested on his shoulder, his arm cradling her. Startled, she twisted to look up at him, but he gently pushed her head back down on his shoulder. "This is more comfortable," he told her before pointing at the screen. "Shh, the movie's starting."

He's right, Frankie thought as she wriggled slightly and stretched out her legs on the sofa cushions. *This is very comfortable.* His chest was warm and solid against her side, his arm draped around her enclosed her in a warm cocoon of male heat and his shoulder was the perfect cushion for her head.

"You still have freckles," he murmured a few moments later, trailing a fingertip over the bridge of her nose.

She tilted her head back to look up and found him watching her instead of the television screen. "You noticed I had freckles?" she asked, surprised.

"Of course." He looked faintly insulted. "You were a cute little kid with a little spray of freckles just over your nose and your cheekbones."

His head lowered, and he brushed soft, tasting kisses over her face, following the arch of her cheekbone. Frankie's breath caught.

"I've wanted to do that for a while," he murmured as he drew back a few inches.

"Have you?" she whispered. His thick, dark lashes were half lowered as he cupped her chin in his palm and stroked his thumb over her cheek. She shivered.

The faintly rough pad of his thumb moved against her sensitive skin, stirring heat in her midsection. His lashes lifted, his gaze leaving her mouth and lifting to meet hers. Desire, hot and alive, lit his eyes. Her skin warmed, flushing under his stare.

"Eli, I don't want to mistake what's happening here." Her voice was a soft murmur. "We agreed to pretend we're attracted to each other to fool Harry—but at the moment, he's not here. It's just the two of us."

"Frankie," he muttered, his fingertips trailing down her throat. "Just so we're clear—this has nothing to do with Harry." His gaze flicked to the base of her throat, where his thumb stroked over the fast race of her pulse. "I want you."

His blunt words widened Frankie's eyes and sent heat flooding through her body. "Eli, I don't—"

He stopped her with a fingertip across her lips. "I'm not saying I want out of our deal to fool Harry. I just want you to know that if I'm kissing you—" he paused, his eyes going hotter "—or anything else physical, I'm not acting."

Frankie's gaze searched his face but found only sincere, focused intent. Much as she was tempted to tell him she wanted him, too, she was scared to death of opening that door. Desire warred with a deep conviction that she needed to protect her heart.

But if she wanted to move past her schoolgirl crush, maybe she needed to be a little more daring. Perhaps limited lovemaking with Eli would inoculate her against another full-blown crush, she thought.

Or maybe she was rationalizing because she desperately wanted more of his kisses. Whatever it was, Frankie decided to take a chance.

"Okay," she murmured. He didn't move, his gaze fixed on hers. Although his thumb continued to stroke seductively against her throat, he clearly waited for her to respond further. She'd never had a conversation quite like this with any man she'd dated but decided to be equally blunt with him. "I'm not ready to sleep with you yet."

"All right."

His body had tensed with her words, his restraint palpable as he waited.

She slipped her arms around his neck, her fingers testing the heavy silk of his dark hair. "Just so we're clear, when we're alone, I'm not pretending, either. And I'm sure I'm ready for more kissing." His muscles tightened against hers. "Maybe some serious fooling around?" she ventured.

A half smile tilted his lips. "I'll take whatever I can get," he murmured before he lifted her, settling her across his lap, and his mouth took hers.

When Eli left Frankie's condo several hours later, he was aroused and hungry, but he'd managed to keep his vow to honor Frankie's decision not to make love.

How the hell he'd kept from seducing her on the sofa, or the carpet or any other available flat surface, he had no idea. He couldn't remember the last time he'd wanted a woman this badly, nor when he'd been so turned on just by kissing.

He drove home and went to bed, but his dreams were hot and vividly sexual.

And all of them featured making love with Frankie.

After one last sizzling good-night kiss, Frankie closed the door behind Eli and slumped against the wood panels. When she straightened, she caught a glimpse of herself in the mirror. Her hair was disheveled and tumbled to her shoulders; her mouth was deeply pink and faintly swollen from the pressure of Eli's lips; her eyes were heavy-lidded and her skin flushed.

She'd barely managed to keep from begging him to make love to her, and if he'd pushed, she wasn't sure she could have said no.

Which meant she needed to decide how she felt about him while he wasn't in the same room, because she obviously lost the ability to think clearly when he was kissing her.

She needed to talk to her sisters, badly.

Frankie picked up the phone and tapped in half the numbers for Tommi before she remembered to look at the clock.

Ten-thirty. On a Friday night. She couldn't call her sister this late. Tommi was five months' pregnant, probably exhausted from a long day at her thriving restaurant and, if she was lucky, her guy was rubbing her feet and feeding her chocolates right about now.

Since Max adored Tommi, Frankie was pretty sure

he was taking good care of her sister, and she didn't want to disrupt their time together. Tommi deserved to be cherished and coddled.

She'd talked to Georgie at work earlier that day and knew she had plans to go out that evening.

And that left Bobbie—but Frankie suspected her younger sister and her new husband were also probably engaged in newlywed bliss at the moment.

Where are the Fairchild women when I need them? She sighed and returned the phone to its base. Her two younger sisters were dizzy with happiness, partnered with men who adored them. Frankie couldn't be happier for them.

But having her sisters busy left Frankie with no one to confide in.

Sighing, she walked into the bathroom. A few moments later, she'd changed into pajamas and climbed into bed, switching off the lamp to stare at the dark ceiling.

Suddenly, she sat bolt upright.

Lily, she realized with delight. She could talk to Lily about Eli. Not only had Lily gone through turmoil before she and Justin had worked out their difficulties to happily marry, but she also knew Eli very well.

She was scheduled to have a playdate with Ava the following morning. They'd arranged to meet at Lily's boutique in Ballard—she could arrive early and, hopefully, have a private conversation with Lily before Justin dropped off Ava.

Relieved that she had a plan, Frankie closed her eyes. Her evening with Eli continued to replay itself behind her lowered eyelids, however, and it was some time before she finally fell asleep.

Chapter Eight

The following morning, she drove to Princess Lily's Boutique a full hour before the time she'd agreed to meet Ava, stopping at a Starbucks in downtown Ballard on her way.

She breathed a sigh of relief when Lily's assistant told her Lily was in the workroom on the second floor. Frankie climbed the stairs and knocked on the open door of the big workspace.

Dressed in slim black slacks, ballet flats and a loose, chic black-and-white patterned top, Lily leaned over the wide table, shears moving swiftly and smoothly as she cut fabric. She glanced over her shoulder at Frankie's knock, a smile lighting her face.

"Frankie! You're here—come in."

"I hope I'm not interrupting you."

"Not at all." Lily's dark hair brushed her shoulders as she shook her head. "I'm glad you could come by early—it seems as if we hardly ever get to chat. We can catch up while we're waiting for Justin to drop off Ava."

"What an excellent idea." Frankie handed Lily a take-out Starbucks cup. "It's green tea," she assured her when Lily lifted a questioning eyebrow. "I thought we'd switch to tea for a while. I considered chai tea," she said, perching on a stool next to Lily's, one of several ranged along the edges of the long worktable that filled the center of the room, "but wasn't sure if you liked the black pepper and spices."

"I'm not a big fan," Lily said. "But I love green tea—so thanks for thinking of me." She leaned a hip against the wide cutting table where a roll of apricot silk snuggled against a half-unrolled bolt of cobalt blue. "I had the distinct impression when you called this morning that this wasn't a spur-of-the-moment visit."

"No," Frankie admitted. "I need a woman's perspective about something, and I can't talk to my sisters about it."

Lily's eyes widened. "And you came to me?" She pulled a stool closer and perched on it, her expression pleased. "I'm all ears." She glanced at her watch. "And we have at least an hour before Justin drops off Ava for your playdate."

"It's about Eli—and me."

"Ahh." Lily nodded sagely. "I heard you two have been dating."

"Yes—we have," Frankie confirmed. She was silent for a moment, tugging on the end of her ponytail.

"And?" Lily prompted when the silence stretched.

"Well…" Frankie drew a deep breath. "Here's the thing. When we started dating, we agreed that it would be…uncomplicated." She was having a difficult time finding the words to make Lily understand without confessing the entire scheme to trick Harry.

"Uncomplicated? As in—you were just friends?" Lily asked.

"Yes, sort of." Frankie sipped her tea and frowned.

"And that's become a problem?" Lily nudged.

"Exactly." Frankie rubbed her fingertips against her temple. "Will you promise not to tell Justin about this?"

"Of course," Lily said firmly.

"Good," Frankie said with relief. "Because he and Eli are such good friends, and I don't want him telling Eli about our conversation."

"I totally understand," Lily assured her.

"So, here's the thing. Since Eli and I have been dating, I'm finding it increasingly difficult to say no to him. It's not that other men haven't wanted to go to bed with me, but…this is *Eli*." Frankie spread her hands expressively, the take-out cup of tea tilting precariously in one hand. "He's practically part of my extended family. If I sleep with him and things don't work out, it's not as if I can just walk away. I'll keep running into him at family gatherings. I'll hear about him in casual conversation from Justin or Uncle Harry."

"I see your problem," Lily said slowly, sipping her tea.

"Not to mention the fact that he hasn't said a word about where he thinks our relationship is going," Frankie added.

Lily's sable eyebrows lifted. "Do you want it to go somewhere? Permanently, I mean?"

Frankie's mouth drooped. "I don't know. I've never wanted a permanent relationship." She slipped off the stool and paced across the room to stare out the bank of tall windows that looked out on Ballard Avenue. Traffic hummed along the brick street below. "But with Eli, I find myself wondering if having a man in my life for the long haul might not be a bad thing."

"Are you saying you've thought marriage was a bad thing up until now?" Lily asked, her voice gentle.

"Maybe not bad," Frankie told her. "Just…not something I could see myself choosing."

"You mean, before Eli?"

"I never thought about it before Eli."

"Ah." Lily nodded and sipped her tea.

"Has it been worth it for you? I mean—" Frankie waved her hand to encompass the high-ceilinged, well-appointed workroom with its bright bolts of silk, mannequins and lingerie-design sketches tacked on the white-painted walls "—you were a successful designer before you met Justin and had Ava. It must have been difficult to readjust your life to include a husband and child."

"Oh, yes." Lily's face softened, her eyes warm as her

gaze met Frankie's. "But their presence in my life has made me a better designer. And even more importantly, a happier, more contented, more fulfilled person."

"Hmm," Frankie murmured, considering Lily's words.

"You and Eli haven't had any conversations, even a few comments, about where your relationship is going?" Lily asked.

Frankie shook her head. "No. We've only been seeing each other for a short time." She paced away from her abandoned stool and Lily, then turned to pace back, too restless to be still. "That's one of the things that bothers me. How can I feel so strongly about him after only a few weeks—days, really," she amended.

"But haven't you known him a long time?"

"Yes, since I was a little girl," Frankie conceded. "But still…" She stopped, leaned a hip against the worktable, and eyed Lily. "Eli Wolf is handsome, charming and kisses like the devil himself. I'm incredibly attracted to him. But he has a reputation for serial dating. He scares me—and I don't know what to do about him."

Lily smiled a mischievous, impish grin. "I swear, I felt the same way about Justin. And I never admitted it to a living soul. Kudos to you, Frankie, for being so honest."

"I don't know what good it does me," Frankie grumbled. "It's not making me feel better. I hate not having answers. I'm a woman who treasures a rational, reasonable approach to life. My sisters tell me I'm too brainy and value logic over emotion, but the truth is, I've never found a situation I couldn't resolve through research and rational thinking." She threw up her hands and paced away once more. "And this situation is filled with emotion and too little logic. He's making me crazy. And on top of everything else about him that's so incredibly attractive, he doesn't appear to be the slightest bit intimidated that I have a PhD in English Lit and two master's degrees. I've never dated a man who didn't ultimately resent me for having a double master's in math and science. It's as if men are offended by a female who likes math or science, but Eli doesn't seem to care in the slightest."

"So, you're saying Eli sees you as a woman, not a brain?"

Frankie thought for a moment, eyes narrowed, before nodding abruptly. "I suppose I am."

Lily's laugh was infectious. "Frankie, do you realize you have the opposite problem from most pretty women—and you are *definitely* pretty," she said firmly. "In any event—" she waved a hand before continuing "—women are more likely to complain that men notice their face and body first, while ignoring their brain. You, on the other hand, appreciate Eli because he sees past your brain to the wonderful woman you are."

"I suppose you're right," Frankie murmured, considering Lily's words.

"I know I'm right," Lily said firmly. "And how terrific is it that Eli appreciates your emotional, physical self and accepts the cerebral, brilliant side of you as well?"

"I think that's part of why I'm so drawn to him," Frankie admitted.

Clear childish tones sounded in the stairwell, answered by a deep male voice as footsteps clattered on the stairs.

"I think Ava's arrived," Lily told her.

The little dark-haired girl burst through the doorway, followed by Justin. Lily's smile held warm affection as she bent to swing Ava up for a hug. The glance she exchanged with Justin as he bent and brushed a kiss against her mouth was filled with love. A twist of wistful envy swept Frankie.

Could she have that with Eli? Was it possible?

"Hi, cousin." Justin threw an arm around her shoulders and gave her a quick, hard hug. "How's everything?"

"Fine, Justin, just fine. How are you?"

He gave her a wry grin. "I've just spent an hour eating pancakes with Ava at Vera's Restaurant. My ears hurt from all the chattering."

Frankie laughed. "That's what you get for having a bright, precocious daughter. When are you going to have a little boy so your family balances the male-female ratio?"

Justin looked at Lily, lifting an eyebrow. "I'll let Lily field that question," he said dryly.

"And Lily's not talking," his wife said with a laugh.

"Good for you," Frankie told them. "Don't cave in to peer pressure. Have a baby when you're ready."

"I'm ready," Ava piped up. "I want a baby brother."

The adults blinked before exchanging glances and laughing.

A half hour later, Frankie and Ava left Lily and Justin in the design room above the boutique to drive to the park for an hour of play.

"Cousin Frankie, can we ride our bikes over there?" Ava pointed at open space in the parking lot behind them.

"Well, we could," Frankie acknowledged. "But if we follow the path around the park, we can stop and get hot chocolate at the coffee stand halfway around."

"Ooh." Ava's eyes lit with anticipation. "Let's go on the path."

"Yes, let's." Frankie unloaded their bikes from the back of the SUV she'd borrowed from Lily. She tucked the keys into the pocket of her black fleece jacket and pushed her bike beside Ava's little pink and white bicycle with its two-toned training wheels as they set off down the path that wound through the Ballard green space. The park was geared toward family activities, and even on this chilly January day, with a brisk breeze tangling hair and turning cheeks pink, the space was thronged. Parents accompanied children as they rode bicycles, tricycles and scooters along the paths, slid down slides or glided high on swings. Bundled up in boots, jeans, fleeces zipped to just beneath their chins, with gloves on their hands and earmuffs to keep their ears warm, Ava and Frankie joined the other children and adults on the wide, paved bike path.

Ava concentrated on pedaling and keeping her wheels

straight, the tip of her pink tongue just visible between her teeth as she focused. The loquacious little girl couldn't be silent for long, however.

"Cousin Frankie, you have to come to my house and see my bunny."

"I heard you have a new rabbit," Frankie told her. "What color is he?"

"He's white with brown spots." Ava wobbled to a stop and looked up, her eyes sparkling. "And he has brown ears!"

"Wow, brown ears? He sounds beautiful," Frankie said gravely.

"And he's really a big bunny," Ava confided. "Daddy says he's a flop-ear."

"Flop-ear?" Frankie repeated, nonplussed. "Oh, you mean a lop-ear?"

"Yes, and he has floppy ears, so I call him flop-ear." Ava beamed.

"Is that his name?"

"No, his name is Mr. Bunny."

"That sounds like a perfect name for a rabbit," Frankie said, hiding a smile.

"I think so, too." Ava nodded emphatically. She pushed determinedly on the pedals, struggling to set the bicycle in motion.

"Can I give you a push?" Frankie asked. "Just till you get going," she added hastily, well aware Ava was currently passionately committed to doing all things by herself, with no adult assistance.

"I guess that's okay." Her little legs pumped when

Frankie moved the bike forward, and once again they were on their way. "Riding bikes is hard," she confided to Frankie. "But now that I'm a big girl, I can steer really good."

"Yes," Frankie agreed solemnly. "I can see that."

"Look!" Ava stopped pedaling and pointed down the path. "It's Unca Eli."

Frankie's gaze followed the direction indicated by Ava's chubby little index finger. Sure enough, Eli was strolling toward them. He wore faded jeans, tennis shoes and a dark blue pullover fleece over a white T-shirt. The breeze tousled his black hair; his cheeks were pink from the cool air. As he drew nearer, his lips curved in a smile, and Frankie felt her heart soar as he reached them.

"Hi, Unca Eli." Ava grinned up at him, and he tousled her hair.

"Nice earmuffs, Ava," he told her, eyeing the hot pink headware.

"Thanks." She beamed and pointed at Frankie. "Cousin Frankie has some just like mine. We match."

"I see." Eli's gaze skimmed over Frankie's hair and met her gaze. "Nice earmuffs, Frankie." His words were so unconnected to the heated message she saw in his eyes that Frankie didn't react for a moment.

"Umm, thanks," she murmured. She glanced sideways at Ava, and the dizzying swirl of mental images, memories of being in his arms last night, dissipated. "What are you doing in the park this morning?" she asked, her voice perfectly steady and normal once more.

"I talked to Justin earlier, and he said you were riding bikes with Ava, so I thought I'd join you," he replied, his eyes lit with amused acknowledgment.

"But you don't have a bike," she pointed out reasonably.

"True." He glanced at Ava. "I'll have to jog to keep up with you. Unless you're training for the Olympics this morning—are you racing this morning, kid?"

The little girl giggled. "No!"

"Whew." He pretended to wipe sweat from his brow with his forearm. "That's a relief. Because if you were racing, I wouldn't have a prayer of keeping up with you—since you're a speed demon!"

He snatched the little girl up and held her suspended over his head as she giggled and squealed. Just as swiftly as he'd picked her up, he planted a smacking kiss on her cheek and lowered her back onto the bike seat.

"I'm ready to jog," he said to Frankie, as if the quick, noisy moment with Ava had never happened.

"I doubt you'll need to run to keep up," she said dryly, bending to give Ava a little push to set her bike wheels in motion. "We're taking it slow and enjoying the moment, aren't we, Ava?"

"Yup." Ava veered sideways before laboriously straightening her handlebars and forging slowly ahead.

Frankie walked beside Eli, pushing her bike as they followed a few steps behind Ava.

"We're stopping for hot chocolate at the refreshment stand just at the halfway point," Frankie told him, pointing at the cream-and-blue wooden building just visible over the heads of a group of teenagers on bikes.

"Do they have coffee?" Eli asked, his expression hopeful.

"Yes, I'm sure they do." Frankie saw his face lighten and laughed. "Not enough caffeine yet this morning?"

"Not enough caffeine since I went to a job site at 4:00 a.m.," he told her.

"Ouch, that's early." She winced in sympathy. "More problems with flooding?"

"Not yet, but I'm worried there might be." Eli briefly explained there was an unstable slope caused by clear-cutting the timber above his construction site. "We're all praying the retaining wall is finished before there's any serious flooding."

"Can't the owner of the lot above yours fix this?" Frankie frowned. "It seems unfair for you and your brothers to suffer damages for his negligence."

Eli shrugged. "That's life in the construction business."

"It still doesn't sound reasonable," Frankie said.

He caught the end of her ponytail and tugged gently, his smile warm. "You're probably right."

"Cousin Frankie," Ava piped up, interrupting them. "Time for hot chocolate."

Frankie realized they'd reached the Blue Hat coffee stand.

"Yes, it is," she agreed. They wheeled their bikes off the path.

Eli plucked Ava off her pink vinyl seat and settled

her on his shoulders. Frankie left her bike next to Ava's, and they joined the line in front of the window.

"What are you doing tonight?" Eli asked her as they waited.

"I'm taking my mom to the Pops symphony at Benaroya Hall. I bought the tickets last fall when they first went on sale."

"Sounds like fun," Eli said. He quirked an eyebrow at her. "Is that your favorite kind of music?"

"Not my favorite, but I like going to the symphony. What's your favorite music?" She eyed him. "Let me guess—some heavy-metal rock band."

"Nah, I like classic rock, like the Stones and Leonard Cohen."

They compared artists they liked, finding they agreed more than they disagreed as the line moved forward until it was their turn to place their order. Moments later, they carried hot take-out cups to a nearby picnic table.

"Come on, Ava-wave-a, time to get off." Eli set his cup down and swung the little girl off his shoulders, depositing her on the bench seat.

"Thanks." She beamed up at him when he handed her a cup of chocolate. "Want to know what my bunny did last night?" she asked, clearly expecting him to say yes.

Eli shot a quick, amused smile at Frankie as he slid onto the bench opposite her and Ava before answering. "Absolutely," he told her.

"Well…" Ava launched into a description of her father

and mother chasing the bunny around the house after he'd escaped when she'd left the cage door open. "Mama says she's going to have you put a lock on the bunny-castle door, Unca Eli. With a key and everything." Her rosebud lips drooped. "But Daddy says he's going to keep the key."

"I see." Eli coughed and covered his mouth.

Frankie was sure he was covering a laugh. *He's so good with her,* she thought. Ava clearly adored him, and, just as clearly, she'd spent a lot of time with him, because she treated him with all the ease and comfort of family.

He'd make a wonderful father. Startled by the thought, she coughed and lifted her cup, sipping the hot chocolate to clear her throat. *Where did that come from?*

It was nearly lunchtime when the three completed the loop of the park and reached the SUV and the parking lot once more.

Eli loaded the two bikes into the back of the SUV while Frankie snapped the latches to secure Ava in her car seat.

"Bye, Ava." He leaned in and gave her a kiss, accepting a chocolate-flavored smack on his cheek in return. He tapped his forefinger against the end of the little girl's nose and closed the door.

"Have fun tonight," he said, holding the door while Frankie slid behind the wheel.

"I will. What are you doing this evening—do you have plans?" she asked, latching her seat belt.

"I'm supposed to have dinner with a college friend, but he hasn't called to confirm, so I might not." He shrugged. "Maybe I'll rent a DVD and order in."

"I wish I had another ticket—you could join us at the symphony," she said.

"Thanks, but you two will enjoy it more without a critic along. Drive carefully." He stepped back and closed the door, waving as they drove away.

Much as Frankie had looked forward to this evening, she couldn't help wishing Eli would be there, too. Activities seemed infused with a certain energy and heightened interest when he was present.

Eli drove away from the park, heading back to the job site. He figured he probably didn't need to double-check the slope again, since it was barely one o'clock and the weather had been clear and cold with no rain since five that morning. Nevertheless, it was second nature for him to be cautious, especially when Wolf Construction had so much time, effort and money invested in the project.

As he'd hoped, the work site was wet from last night's rain, but no further damage had occurred. Eli headed across I-5, on his way to Ballard and his grandfather's home.

"Hey, Granddad," Eli called, rapping his knuckles on the back door as he stepped through it and into the kitchen. He'd grown up in the rambling old house on Sixty-fifth Street, blocks away from historic Larson's Bakery in Ballard. When their parents were killed in an accident, Jack Wolf had taken his four grandsons into his home. Now the big house was once more occupied only by the veteran carpenter, since Eli and his brothers each lived in their own place.

"Is that you, Eli?" Jack's gravelly voice grew louder and he entered the kitchen from the living room. He beamed. "Haven't seen much of you lately. Where you been keepin' yourself?" He waved a gnarled hand at the kitchen table with its red plaid oilcloth cover. "Sit down, I just made a pot of coffee."

"Coffee sounds great, Granddad." Eli deposited the bag of chocolate-covered donuts on the table and shrugged out of his jacket, hanging it on the back of an oak chair. He pulled the chair out and sat, stretching his long legs out to cross them at the ankles.

Jack carried two mugs to the table, his eyes lighting when he saw the bag. "You stopped at Larson's Bakery? I always knew I liked you the best of my four grandsons."

Eli chuckled. "You say the same thing to whichever one of us brings you donuts from Larson's."

"Well, yeah, I do." Jack set a mug in front of Eli and took the seat across the table. "But then, whoever brings me something from Larson's, that's the boy I like the best. At least for the moment," he added with a twinkle in his eyes.

Eli opened the bag, took out a donut and passed the bag to Jack. "Then I suppose I'll enjoy my favorite-grandson status, for the moment."

"Wise of you." Jack accepted the bag and squinted

into it before grunting his approval and removing a chocolate-covered donut. "What are you doing at my house on a Saturday afternoon?" he asked before taking a bite.

"I had to check a job site for flooding, and since I had to drive by the bakery, I stopped to pick up donuts."

"The condo building over by the university?" Jack asked, his eyes narrowing.

Eli nodded. "Yeah, that's the one. The owner clear-cut the trees off the slope above it, so every time it rains, there's the potential for trouble."

"You're putting in drains to take care of the problem long-term, aren't you?"

"Yeah, but they aren't finished, and until they are, I'm keeping a close eye on the site."

Jack nodded. "Good call. I once lost a whole six-story building, just days away from completion, when a bad storm soaked the slope above it. Four big cedar trees uprooted and slid down the hill, taking everything on the slope with them. That landslide slammed into the retaining wall, took out the back of the building and destabilized the whole shebang." Jack shook his head at the memory. "What a waste. We had to tear down the building and get the ground stabilized before we could rebuild. Your dad was mad as a hornet over that one."

"I bet the insurance company wasn't happy, either," Eli commented.

"Nope, they weren't." Jack finished his donut and took another from the sack. "That was a pretty woman who came looking for you the other day."

Eli glanced sideways to find Jack eyeing him, curiosity gleaming in his blue eyes.

"Yes," he agreed. "She's pretty."

"You two been keeping company for a while?"

"Not too long."

"You met her folks yet?"

Eli shot a sharp glance at his grandfather, but Jack only stared back, an innocent expression on his features.

"Justin introduced me to her mother years ago, and her father died when Frankie was young."

"Hmm." Jack narrowed his eyes thoughtfully. "Seems to me I remember you mentioning Justin Hunt being kinda protective of his cousin Frankie."

"Yeah, so?"

"So how does your best friend feel about you dating his favorite cousin?"

Eli shrugged. "I don't know. We haven't talked about it."

"Seems to me you better have an answer. Justin ran wild in this house when you two were kids, so I'm thinking I know him pretty well. He's likely to demand to know your intentions toward her. You'd better be ready with the right answer, or there's likely to be trouble."

"Justin's not going to go off half-cocked," Eli growled, shooting a frown at his grandfather. "He knows me better than that."

"Huh." Jack snorted. "He knows you've never had a permanent woman in your life, that's what he knows."

"What's that got to do with it?" Eli demanded.

"You and Justin were bachelors for a long time, so you know each other's habits well. He's not going to want you sleeping with his cousin for a while, then moving on to the next female," Jack said bluntly.

"Damn, Granddad." Insulted, Eli stared at him. "You think I'm not capable of having anything more than a temporary connection with a woman?"

"No. Hell, no." Jack shook his head emphatically. "I'm just sayin' that up until now, you haven't had anything close to permanent. That's all."

Eli stared moodily at his coffee mug, turning it in slow circles on the red and white oilcloth. "Yeah, well… maybe that's changed."

"Yeah?" Jack's eyebrows rose in surprise. "If that's true, I'm glad to hear it. Up until now, none of you boys have showed any signs you might be considering settling down. I'd be happy if you were thinking about something permanent with Frankie."

"I'm not saying I am, and I'm not saying I'm not," Eli told him.

"What *are* you sayin'?" Jack asked testily.

Eli looked up and met his grandfather's blue eyes, fierce beneath lowered white brows.

"If I were looking to settle down, Frankie's the kind of woman I'd be looking for." Eli saw the old man's eyebrows shoot upward and his eyes light with glee. "But I'm not looking for a woman to settle down with."

"Hmph." Jack snorted and grabbed another donut. "You don't make any sense."

Eli wasn't sure he was making sense, either, but he'd

be damned if he'd tell his granddad. "Yeah, well, I'm only thirty-five. Statistics say lots of men in today's world don't get married until they're forty. They're busy building careers first."

Jack's hmph of disgust clearly conveyed his opinion of the statistics and the reasoning behind them. "Your daddy and mama were married when they were barely twenty years old, both of them. And your daddy had a family while we were both busy building the company." Jack leveled a finger at Eli. "And don't tell me you're not glad we kept Wolf Construction afloat during those early hard years, 'cause I know you like running it. And if we could both juggle families and working, you and your brothers could, too." He nodded emphatically and reached for another donut.

"You're right. I like running Wolf Construction." Eli didn't think it would help to tell his granddad that he'd spent a couple of hours in the park with Frankie and Ava earlier. Nor that watching her with Ava had made him wonder what it would be like if the little girl were their child.

Frankie would make a wonderful mother. She was great with Ava, affectionate and warm but firm when needed.

The sudden mental image of a little girl with Frankie's blond hair and brown eyes, one that called him daddy, had stunned him. He hadn't been able to get that image out of his mind.

But damned if he was going to confess that to Jack.

The old man would never give him any peace if he knew he was imagining having children with Frankie.

"I'm starting to wonder if any of you boys will ever get married and give me great-grandchildren to take fishing," Jack growled.

"What?" Startled, Eli's attention snapped back to his grandfather. Had the old man been reading his mind?

"I'd like some kids in this family," Jack told him bluntly. "It's been too long since we've had little ones around."

"Justin's dad felt that way and tried to force his sons to marry and have kids," Eli reminded him. "Don't take a page from Harry's playbook—he's lucky his sons are still speaking to him after he threatened to sell HuntCom."

"Wouldn't work with you and your brothers," Jack said regretfully. "You've already inherited your dad's sixty percent of Wolf Construction." He eyed Eli speculatively. "I suppose I could threaten to sell my forty percent to an outside party if you four don't get married soon and have some babies."

"Don't even think about it," Eli said mildly, sipping his coffee.

Jack laughed. "Might be worth it, just to make you all a little crazy." His eyes twinkled.

"Connor might have a heart attack," Eli told him. "Just remember—" he pointed his index finger at Jack "—paybacks are hell."

"That's true." Jack heaved a loud sigh and took another doughnut from the bag.

"Damned straight." Eli nodded emphatically. He wondered why the thought of getting married and having kids didn't seem as inconceivable as usual.

He doubted it was coincidence that listening to Jack talk about marriage and babies led directly to Technicolor mental images of Frankie.

Eli could handle lusting after her. Any healthy male with a libido would react the same to the beautiful blonde.

No, what shook him were the unfamiliar feelings of possessiveness and the gut-deep need to claim and protect.

He'd never felt this level of emotion for a woman before. If he were a man who believed in fate, he'd suspect he'd met his match in Frankie Fairchild and life as he knew it had been changed forever.

Chapter Nine

On Sunday afternoon, the day after biking in the park with Eli and Ava, Frankie met two of her sisters to shop at Pacific Place in downtown Seattle. Tommi was busy with Max and couldn't join them, but Bobbie, Georgie and Frankie happily browsed racks of sweaters, slacks and jeans, then tried on shoes before gathering for lunch at one of their favorite spots, the Nordstrom café.

"It looks like Bobbie has the most bags," Frankie said, stowing her single bag containing a lime-green cashmere sweater with matching hat and gloves under her chair.

"I found shoes on sale," Bobbie replied, delighted. "Fabulous prices—I couldn't resist."

"I bought a pair of black heels," Georgie put in. "I'm

looking forward to shopping in New York and didn't plan to buy a thing today but I couldn't resist them."

"I also hit the lingerie section." Bobbie swung a light bag from one finger, her smile slightly wicked. "Gabe is going to love what I bought."

"Show us," Frankie demanded, knowing her sister's smile meant she planned to seduce her fiancé.

Bobbie opened the bag and tugged out just enough black lace over cream satin to make her sisters ooh and ah before tucking the bag beneath her chair with her purse.

The waiter arrived with their order, placed earlier at the long counter in the entry room, and it was several moments before conversation resumed.

"Can you believe Mom?" Frankie asked, stirring a teaspoonful of sugar into her tea. "I wonder if she's serious about the golf pro at the club?"

"I doubt it." Georgie shook her head.

Frankie wasn't so sure. She noted the unconvinced expression on Bobbie's face and looked back at Georgie. "Why don't you think this might be serious—is it because he's so much younger than her?"

"That—and I can't see Mom remarrying," Georgie said. "Look how long she's been single." She took a bite of her club sandwich.

"I don't know," Bobbie put in. "I'm a firm believer in a woman's right to change her mind about living alone. Tommi and I did."

"Yes, but you're a lot younger than Mom," Georgie pointed out.

"True," Bobbie conceded.

"But Mom looks and acts so much younger than her real age," Frankie argued. "I swear, she seems younger than most fifty-year-olds."

"Which is probably why Greg is so taken with her," Bobbie pointed out.

"I wonder if Mom realizes she's now doing what she always told Harry he *shouldn't* do when he dated younger women," Frankie said with a grin, filled with amusement that sixty-six-year-old Cornelia was dating a man of forty-nine.

"I'm not brave enough to tell her." Bobbie's eyes twinkled as she sipped her green tea.

"Me, either!" Frankie said promptly, her words immediately echoed by Georgie.

"Speaking of dating," Georgie said, fixing Frankie with a curious look. "I hear you went out with Eli Wolf."

Frankie nodded, well aware that Bobbie had stopped eating and was staring at her with surprise.

"I didn't know you were going out with Eli," Bobbie told her. "When did this happen?"

"We went to the Children's Hospital fundraiser last Saturday," Frankie said.

"Are you seeing him again?" Bobbie asked.

"Tomorrow night," Frankie responded. "He's taking me to his favorite bar to meet his brothers and have dinner."

"It sounds as if the two of you are spending a lot of time together," Georgie commented.

Frankie shrugged. "Just a few dates. I won't see him the rest of the week because he and his brother Connor are flying to Las Vegas for a business conference on Tuesday and won't be back till late Sunday night."

She didn't miss the significant glance Bobbie exchanged with Georgie.

"What?" she demanded.

"For someone who's had only 'a few dates,' it certainly sounds as if the two of you are an item," Georgie said.

Bobbie leaned forward, fixing her with a sober stare. "What about the physical side? Are you compatible?"

"He's an incredible kisser." Frankie's gaze went slightly unfocused as she remembered their heated kisses. "I haven't slept with him," she said bluntly, "but I'm guessing it would just as amazing."

"You haven't slept with him?" Georgie's eyes went wide.

"No." Frankie shook her head. "Why do you sound so surprised?"

"Because you've apparently been seeing quite a bit of each other and rumor has it, Eli never dates women just for their conversation."

"Hmm." Frankie had heard those same rumors. "I'm not likely to get involved with a man who'll break my heart," she told them. "Not to worry."

Bobbie and Georgie looked unconvinced but didn't protest when Frankie asked Georgie a question about her upcoming assignment that would take her to New York City for several months.

She was relieved when the conversation turned away from her and Eli. Because the truth was, she had to admit Eli Wolf was much more than she'd anticipated— more attractive, more charming, more seductive. Added to that, she was finding she simply liked the man he was.

And that was perhaps the most dangerous thing of all.

The following Monday evening, Eli picked up Frankie and drove to Killoran's Pub in Ballard. Tucked into a brick side street off Ballard Avenue, the pub had been the Wolf brothers' favorite place to play pool, listen to live music, drink beer and grab a hot sandwich or pizza since they'd turned twenty-one.

"I can't stay too late," Frankie told Eli as he held the heavy door for her. "I have an early class in the morning."

"I'll have you home before ten," he promised.

They stepped inside and paused, met with a wave of conversation and laughter. The yeasty smell of beer and bread mixed with the scent of pizza in the walnut-paneled room.

"Hey, Eli, back here," Connor yelled from a table halfway to the rear of the long, narrow room.

Eli lifted a hand in acknowledgment and tucked Frankie under his arm. Together they wound their way between crowded tables toward his brothers.

Several times they were stopped when someone

caught Eli's arm, halting him to say hello and exchange a few words before they could move on.

"You know lots of people here," Frankie said, leaning up to speak close to his ear so he could hear her over the noise.

He nodded. "I've been coming here after work for years. A lot of these guys have worked on jobs with me."

At last, they reached the table. Eli pulled out chairs for them, seating Frankie before dropping into the chair next to her.

"Man, it's crowded in here tonight," he commented, holding Frankie's black raincoat as she shrugged out of the sleeves.

"Michael O'Shea is playing later," Ethan told him. "He has a lot of fans."

"Yeah, and they're all crammed into this room," Matt added dryly. He lifted a pitcher and poured a glass of beer, passing it to Frankie before filling another for Eli. "Have you two eaten yet?"

"No. I wanted Frankie to try the grilled Italian sandwich on ciabatta bread."

"Good call." Connor leaned forward to nod. "The pizza is good, too."

"What do you say, Frankie—sandwich or pizza?" Eli asked, stretching his arm along the back of her chair and leaning in so she could hear him over the noise.

"What are you having?" she asked. Her lips brushed his ear as she spoke, and he turned his head to look at her, blue eyes heating. Electricity arced between them, and Frankie caught her breath.

"Sandwich," he murmured against her ear.

Frankie shivered with awareness, his breath stirring the tendrils of hair at her nape. Earlier, she'd pulled her hair up into a ponytail, donned a black cashmere sweater over pencil-thin jeans with boots and slipped gold hoops into her earlobes. The ponytail left her nape bare, and when Eli stroked his thumb over the back of her neck, she realized how very vulnerable she was to his touch.

"How about you?" he asked.

Belatedly, Frankie realized he was waiting for her to answer.

"Oh, me, too," she said. "Whatever you're having."

His lips curved in a brief smile, and Frankie suddenly wished they were alone. She badly wanted his mouth on hers.

On the stage behind them, the microphone screeched. The noise yanked Frankie back to awareness of her surroundings, and she sat forward, reaching for control as she moved away from Eli's disturbing touch. She picked up her glass and sipped her beer, leaning her elbows on the table as Eli stopped a waiter to recite their order and she listened to his brothers arguing.

"…and I'm telling you there's no way that specific gaming software will run as fast as it should on your computer," Ethan said vehemently. "You need more hard-drive capacity."

Frankie blinked. "Your brother is a techno guy?"

she murmured to Eli. "Does he know anything about programming cell phones?"

"Probably," Eli told her. "You have a problem with yours?"

She nodded. "I have a new phone and haven't had time to figure out how to transfer all my numbers and info from my old phone," she explained. "So I'm carrying both of them, because my address book, email addresses, et cetera, are all stored in the original phone. I'd love to get rid of it and just have one."

"I can fix it," Matt put in before Eli could respond. "I'm good with cell phones."

"I'm better," Connor declared. "Besides, I just did that with my new cell. It'll be a piece of cake."

"Don't let either of them touch your phone," Ethan warned her with a slow smile. "They'll break it."

"I'll do it for you," Eli told her. "If you let any of them have your phone, God knows what they'll do to it."

"Oh, come on, Eli," Matt protested. "I programmed all the work cell phones a few months ago, and they all work fine."

"Yeah," Eli said, his voice dry. "And the ring tones were annoying as hell."

Matt grinned at Frankie. "He's just mad because his ringtone was 'Macarena.'"

Frankie sputtered, nearly choking on a mouthful of her drink. Eyes wide, she looked at Eli to find him watching her, a lazy smile on his handsome face. Within moments, though, she joined his brothers, laughing at Eli's disgruntled expression.

"I'm better than my brothers with technical equipment, Frankie. You'd better let me fix your phone," Ethan repeated.

"No." Eli's voice held finality. "I'll do it."

"All right." Frankie opened her purse, shifting through the contents until she found the two cell phones. "Here you are." She handed them to Eli as she dropped her purse at her feet once more. "The new one is the hot-pink one. The old one is the silver."

"Hot pink?" Eli lifted his eyebrows in disbelief. "You have a hot-pink phone? Geez." Eli clearly was speechless. Nonetheless, he started scrolling through her menu.

As Eli concentrated on her phones, the three younger Wolf brothers regaled her with stories of the hours they'd spent in the bar and the musicians who'd appeared on the small stage—some already famous, some who had gone on to become famous. They took turns teasing each other about the women they'd met, won and lost within the four walls.

The waiter interrupted them to slide plates of sandwiches with pickles and chips on the table in front of Frankie and Eli. He deposited a large pizza, loaded with cheese, meat and veggies, in the middle of the table and set plates in front of Ethan, Connor and Matt.

Eli handed Frankie her phones.

"Are you done already?" she asked, startled.

"Yeah," he told her. "I'll explain how I did it later."

"Great." She smiled at him with delight. "Thanks so much. I have no idea when I would have had time to sit down and figure out how to transfer everything. I owe you."

The slow curve of his lips set her heart pounding.

"I'll think of a way for you to pay me," he murmured so only she could hear.

Flushing, Frankie darted a quick look at the others around the table as his smile widened, his eyes gleaming with amusement at her reaction to his flirting. Thankfully, the others were busy loading pizza onto plates.

"Hey, Frankie, do you have any sisters?" Matt asked, his expression hopeful.

"Yes, I do." She sipped her drink, making him wait. "Three, to be exact. But one just got married, the other is in a relationship, and only the third is single. Unfortunately—" she picked up a chip and nibbled "—she's moving to New York City soon."

Matt's face fell. "Damn."

Frankie glanced at Eli. The amusement in his blue eyes echoed her own and when he winked, she laughed.

The evening flew, Eli looking on indulgently as his brothers tried to coax Frankie to introduce them to her friends, teasing her when she demurred and arguing over which one of them should be allowed to take Eli's place and drive her home.

Time flew and all too soon, it was after nine-thirty.

As promised, Eli led Frankie out of the pub early and drove her home.

"I'd love to ask you to come in," she told him after

unlocking her condo door. "But if I do, I won't want you to leave."

"I make a mean omelet," he told her, bracketing her against the closed door panels by planting his palms on each side of her shoulders and leaning close. He brushed a kiss against the corner of her mouth. "And great coffee. I'll feed you breakfast in bed before you leave for work."

Frankie closed her eyes, tilting her head back to give his warm, seductive lips better access to her throat.

"Tempting," she managed to get out. He nudged her coat collar aside and explored the juncture where throat met shoulder. She shivered with longing but planted her palms against the soft fleece covering the hard muscles of his chest, keeping him from pulling her into his arms. "But I really do have to be at work early in the morning."

"I'll drive you to work early," he murmured, lifting his head to look down at her. His eyes were heavy-lidded, the blue irises darkened to navy.

"If you come in and stay, neither one of us will get any sleep tonight," she told him, smiling at the reluctant acceptance she read on his features.

He drew a deep breath, expelling it in a rough sigh.

"You're right. Kiss me, and I'll go home," he growled, pulling her close.

Lips curved in a smile, Frankie wound her arms around his neck and went up on her toes, meeting his mouth with hers, quickly swept away by the passion that flared between them.

When he set her back on her heels, she was dazed, her knees like jelly.

He tucked her hair behind her ear. "Connor and I have an early flight in the morning, but I'll call you from Vegas. The conference lasts through Friday, but we're staying to play a little blackjack and flying home late Sunday."

"I'll miss you," she told him. "Be safe."

"I'll miss you, too. Don't run off with any other guy while I'm gone," he teased. Then he took her mouth in one more swift, hard kiss before he pushed open the door behind her and gently shoved her inside. "Lock the door," he ordered softly as he pulled the door shut.

Frankie twisted the deadbolt closed and slid the chain into its slot. Listening, she didn't hear Eli walk away until after the locks snicked closed. Smiling at his protective patience, she turned and strolled toward her bedroom, dreamily reliving those heartstopping kisses while she got ready for bed.

And when she fell asleep, she dreamed of Eli.

Eli and Connor flew out of Sea-Tac the following morning to attend the contractor's conference in Las Vegas. Although he called Frankie each night, he missed seeing her. Months earlier, when they'd booked the conference, he and Connor had planned to spend the weekend in Vegas after the conference ended on Friday. He wasn't slated to fly back to Seattle until Sunday evening, but on Friday he changed his flight and flew home on the red-eye, reaching home in Seattle just after two in the morning.

The following morning, he was awake by nine, but Frankie didn't answer her cell phone when he called. Fortunately, he reached her sister Tommi at her restaurant and learned Frankie had driven to Arlington, north of Seattle, to spend the day volunteering at a rescue horse stable.

Eli scribbled the directions Tommi gave him on a napkin and headed north up I-5, toward the farm.

He remembered Frankie had briefly mentioned her volunteer work at the barn while telling him anecdotes about her childhood with Cornelia and her sisters. Cornelia had sat Frankie down on her eighth birthday, discussed the responsibility of individuals to contribute to the larger community and asked her to pick a cause to which she would commit her time and energy. Frankie loved horses and had chosen an organization that rescued abused and damaged horses.

That early exposure had become a lifelong devotion to the rescue operation in Arlington. Tommi had told him earlier that Frankie usually left her cell phone in her car when she was at the barns. While disappointed that he couldn't reach her, Eli decided that surprising her in person would be even better.

He left the freeway just past Arlington, turning onto a two-lane road that wound through the countryside, where rolling acres of green pastures held horses and the occasional cow. After twenty minutes of driving past farms and fields, he reached a complex of big barns and fenced pastures. He turned into the wide lane, jolting over bumps and avoiding holes in the graveled road before parking in a large dirt lot.

A huge wooden barn, a round pen with green metal pole fencing and a long low stable were set in a semi-circle around the dirt parking lot.

Eli left his car and walked to the open barn doors, following the sound of voices as he stepped inside. To his left, a flight of stairs led upward, and, hearing voices, he climbed the steps to the second floor. But the office there was empty, as were the bleacher seats that lined the outer walls. He peered over the waist-high divider and down into a huge arena with a soft dirt floor. An older woman in boots and jeans stood in the center of the arena, directing a young girl wearing a riding helmet and snug pants tucked into high boots. She sat atop a rangy thoroughbred that looked too tall and much too big for the small girl. Nevertheless, she handled him with easy confidence.

Eli retraced his steps down the stairs and turned left, following a hallway until it turned sharply right. Ahead of him stretched a wide alley with stalls opening off each side. He started down the alley, stopping to stroke his palm over muzzles as horses looked out over the top of open half doors to nicker and call.

"Back up, Daisy. Stop being so stubborn. You know you can't go outside."

Frankie's annoyed voice reached Eli's ears. He searched the barn ahead of him but didn't see her. A side alley opened to the left just two stalls ahead, and several thuds and bumps sounded as if the noise came from there. Hoping to surprise her, his stride lengthened and he rounded the corner.

Frankie stood at an open stall door only feet away, a halter rope in one hand while the other hand and one shoulder pushed against the side of a massive draft horse.

The huge horse was clearly winning the argument as she took a step forward, her hooves big as dinner plates and planted too close to Frankie's boots.

Cold fear iced Eli's heart. He reached Frankie in three long strides, lifting her out of the way with an arm around her waist.

"W-what on earth…!" Frankie sputtered in surprise.

Busy muscling the big draft horse back into the stall, Eli didn't look at Frankie until he'd slammed the door on the massive horse. Then he turned to face her.

"What the hell do you think you're doing?" he roared.

She stiffened, surprise giving way to anger that flushed her delicate features with color, her brown eyes snapping. "My job," she said succinctly. "What are you doing?"

"Saving your pretty butt," he snapped. "Did you not notice that horse outweighs you by a thousand pounds?"

"More than that," she shot back. "And I fail to see what concern that is of yours."

"Are you crazy? You were about to get stepped on."

Frankie waved a hand at the big horse, who watched them with interested brown eyes from her stall. "I was *not*. Daisy has never stepped on anyone in all the years she's been here. She tries to get out into the paddock whenever someone opens her stall door, but she's perfectly docile. She's never hurt anyone in her life."

"She's so big she wouldn't know if she hurt you," Eli told her, his voice just barely below a roar. "You could have been killed or badly hurt. You're too little—you can't handle a horse that big."

"You don't have the right to tell me what I can or can't do," she told him, fingers curled into fists at her sides.

"Well, someone has to. You clearly don't have sense enough to know you're too damned small to muscle around a horse that's twenty times your size and weight," he growled, anger fueled by the terrifying sight of her pitting her fragile frame against the huge horse.

Her brown eyes shot sparks. "I've been making my own decisions since I was eighteen," she informed him, her voice dripping ice. "And if I was going to give someone permission to interfere in my choices, it would *not* be you. Especially since you clearly know *nothing* about horses," she snarled.

"I don't need to know anything about horses to know this horse—" he jerked a thumb over his shoulder at the stall "—is too damned big for you to push around."

"It's got nothing to do with her size," Frankie yelled, planting her fists on her hips, the air fairly sizzling around her. "She's a Clydesdale and so gentle Ava could handle her. Oh, what's the use? You're impossible." She threw up her hands and turned on her heel.

"Where are you going?" Eli yelled after her.

"Home," she shot over her shoulder as she strode away, her boots kicking up puffs of dust. She stopped abruptly and spun around to glare at him. "And don't follow me. I don't want to talk to you. Not until you realize what an ass you've been and are ready to apologize— and maybe not even then." She spun on her heel once more and stalked off.

Fuming silently, Eli watched her until she disappeared through the door at the end of the alley lined with stalls. He didn't care how mad she was; he was right about this. *And it'll be a cold day in hell before I apologize for trying to keep her safe.*

Thoroughly disgusted and out of sorts, he left the barn. Frankie was nowhere to be seen when he reached the parking lot and drove away.

I should have stayed in Vegas, he told himself as he headed back to Seattle. *I could be sitting at a blackjack table, enjoying myself, instead of wasting my time trying to reason with an irrational woman.*

The first drops of rain hit his windshield. Eli looked at the sky and realized that while he'd been in the barn, the sunny morning had turned dark and cloudy.

"Great," he muttered. "Just great."

Frankie dashed away tears of anger as she drove south toward Seattle. The fact that she was tearing up infuriated her. She'd missed Eli more than she'd thought possible over the last few days and had looked forward to seeing him when he returned.

Then he'd stalked into the barn and like a typical domineering male, assumed she was acting foolishly and set out to save her from her own stupidity.

"Arrogant jerk," she muttered, fingers tightening on the steering wheel.

He hadn't even bothered to ask her—no, he'd all but *told* her she was an idiot for handling Daisy.

"As if I didn't know how big Daisy is," she grumbled to herself. "As if I haven't been shoving Daisy around since she was three months old. But did he ask me anything about her? No, he did not," she answered her own question. "Men," she snarled, eyes narrowing at the windshield. "They're impossible."

A few fat raindrops splatted against the windshield.

Frankie switched on the wipers. *Perfect,* she thought, *just what I needed.*

Traffic slowed with the sudden downpour, taillights winking red as drivers braked.

Frankie groaned and wished she were home, impatient with the delay that gave her far too much time to contemplate how much she wished she'd taken more time to tell Eli Wolf how wrong he was about her ability to handle Daisy. And she should have added how annoying she found it when someone prejudged a situation without first asking questions and gathering facts.

And men think women act irrationally, she thought with a humph of disbelief.

She refused to think about how much she'd been

looking forward to his return from Las Vegas—and how disappointed she felt that anticipation had turned into anger.

With a quick twist, she turned on the radio, filling the car's interior with the sound of upbeat bluegrass music.

The bright music failed to lift the leaden weight that pressed on her chest but she ignored it, determined not to mope because she and Eli had argued.

Chapter Ten

The rain continued all weekend, and Monday brought more gray skies and wet weather.

Tuesday night, Eli drove home from work, parked his truck in the garage and entered his condo through the utility room. He paused to take off his wet, muddy boots and left them on the mat next to the washing machine. Then he shucked off his jeans, soaked and splattered with mud from hem to knees, and dropped them into the empty washer, following them with his wet flannel shirt and socks. Wearing only a white T-shirt and navy boxers, he padded in bare feet into the kitchen, stopping to set the containers of take-out Chinese food he'd bought earlier on the counter before heading upstairs to the bathroom.

Three days had passed since he and Frankie had

argued at the horse barn, and he'd been in a foul mood ever since. His brothers were threatening to ban him from the work trailer.

It's the rain, he told himself. *Anybody would be in a bad mood with three days of gray skies and downpour.*

He turned on the shower, letting the steam warm the tiled area as he stripped out of his boxers and T-shirt.

When he finally stepped into the stall, the enclosure was heated, the pulse of the showerhead hitting him with enough force to make him groan with relief. He shampooed and scrubbed, then let the hot spray of water sluice the suds away. He propped his palms on the tiled wall and let the water beat a rhythm against aching back muscles until it began to cool before he got out.

Drying off, he walked naked into the bedroom to pull on clean boxers, a pair of worn jeans and a soft T-shirt.

His hair was still damp when he went back downstairs, pausing in the living room to switch on the television. In the kitchen, he collected a fork and the thermal containers of takeout, then grabbed a beer from the fridge and returned to the living room.

Outside, the wind howled as the storm continued to dump rain on Seattle. It reminded Eli of the evening he'd spent in Frankie's apartment, curled up next to her on the sofa. He wished he was back there.

Damn. He stared at the TV without seeing it. He missed the hell out of being with Frankie.

He liked his condo, liked his independent life. Since

he'd started seeing Frankie, however, he'd realized that just spending time with her, even if they were only sharing a pizza and watching a movie, felt right—maybe more right than being alone.

It was almost as if a missing piece of his life had fallen into place.

Before dating Frankie, he hadn't even known there *was* a piece of his life missing.

He'd dated a lot of women and enjoyed their company, but dates had always been a precursor to sex. He couldn't remember a time since puberty when just being in a woman's company was enough.

Not that he didn't want to sleep with Frankie. In fact, he suspected he was damned near obsessed with the thought of taking her to bed. He prided himself on his self-control, but he had to admit it was growing increasingly more difficult to stop at kisses and fooling around. Especially since she seemed to find him just as irresistible as he found her.

But he still sensed a certain hesitancy, a kind of wariness in her. With any other woman, he would have tried to charm and seduce her out of whatever was making her hold back. But with Frankie, it was strangely imperative that she choose to come to him willingly, wholeheartedly.

Why it was so, he didn't know. Maybe simply because this was Frankie, and he'd known her since she was a girl. Maybe it was because she was Justin's favorite cousin. Whatever it was, what was happening between

Frankie and him was different from any relationship he'd had with a woman before.

Not that there was anything happening between him and Frankie at the moment, he thought, frowning. She hadn't called him, and he hadn't called her, either. He'd told himself it was because she'd made herself clear before she stalked away from him and out of the barn. She'd said she didn't want to talk to him. He was only being cooperative, giving her time to calm down.

Yeah, right. The real reason he wasn't calling Frankie was because she'd scared the hell out of him at the barn. Seeing the big Clydesdale horse looming over her had made his blood run cold.

I overreacted when I yelled at her. But, damn, what was I supposed to think?

And Frankie was too independent to let him get away with ordering her around. In fact, he doubted she'd ever let anyone tell her what to do—not unless there was a logical reason. And then a person would be wise to suggest, not order or demand.

Hell. He scrubbed his hand down his face and sighed, a deep, gusty sound of frustration. He wasn't very good at taking orders himself. Fate must be howling with laughter. He'd found the one woman he couldn't— didn't—want to live without, and she was just as bloody stubborn and independent as he was.

Stunned, he considered what he'd just thought.

Was he in falling in love with Frankie? Was that what the sleepless nights and foul temper were all about?

He didn't even want to think about it.

Determinedly, he took a bite of chow mein and switched the channel to a basketball game on ESPN.

He couldn't be falling in love.

And even if he was, he thought with a frown, he was damned if he'd keep thinking about it nonstop.

After several hours of slamming pots and pans, then cleaning her condo from top to bottom while listening to Sugarland and Jon Bon Jovi CDs on Saturday afternoon, Frankie's temper settled into a slow simmer.

She'd suspected Eli seemed too perfect to be true, she reflected on Sunday afternoon as she jogged around Green Lake. And sure enough, he'd revealed he was human on Saturday at the barn.

No, not that he's human, she thought with a flash of anger, *that he's a jerk who thinks I'm incapable of making sensible decisions about my safety.*

She jogged faster, pumping her arms, the steady downpour of rain soaking the shoulders of her all-weather jacket. She'd stuffed her hair up under a bright blue wool stocking hat that matched her coat. The hat was damp and so were the black leggings that covered her long legs. Her toes squished inside her running shoes.

It was a measure of how restless and unsettled she was that she'd chosen to face the rain and elements rather than run on the treadmill at home.

After circling the lake twice, she left the wide tarmac path and drove to her mom's house.

"Mom? Are you home?" she called as she stepped

into the glassed-in porch. She toed off her shoes, leaving them to drip on the mat, and padded across the painted board floor to the inner door. Her damp socks left footprints on the flooring.

"Frankie? I'm in the kitchen," Cornelia called.

Frankie hopped on first one foot, then the other, to tug off her wet socks before walking across the beautiful Oriental wool rug and into the kitchen. Cornelia stood at the counter next to the stove, pouring water from a steaming kettle into a china teapot.

"Hi, Mom. Tommi, I didn't see your car outside." She was glad to see her sister. Tommi was perched on a stool at the island in the center of the big kitchen, a bright red maternity smock stretched over her burgeoning tummy.

"Max dropped me off—he's coming back to pick me up in an hour." Tommi's eyes twinkled. "You'd think no other woman had ever been pregnant before. He insists on driving me everywhere—at least, everywhere I'll let him." She grinned, clearly enjoying the coddling.

"For heaven's sake, Frankie," Cornelia looked up from the Wedgwood teapot and returned the kettle to the stove. "You're drenched. What have you been doing?" She threw the question over her shoulder as she disappeared into the half bath just off the kitchen.

"Jogging at Green Lake," Frankie responded.

"Couldn't you have stayed in and used the treadmill?" Tommi asked as Cornelia reappeared with a thick towel.

"Yes, why didn't you?" Cornelia asked, handing over

the towel and taking Frankie's drenched coat. "I'm going to toss this in the dryer," she said, leaving the room again.

Frankie plucked the soggy hat off her head and dropped it on the tile counter next to the sink. "I'm tired of being stuck in the house," she said. "And I'm not made of sugar—I won't melt in the rain."

"Yes, but you might catch your death of cold," Cornelia said, coming back into the room. "Dry off. I've got vitamin C and zinc tablets here."

Frankie and Tommi exchanged a fond glance.

"Thanks, Mom." Frankie knew from experience that it was easier to let Cornelia mother her. She rubbed her face dry and blotted her hair before joining Tommi at the counter, taking a stool directly across from her. "How's everything at the restaurant?"

"Wonderful." Tommi fairly glowed as she brought Frankie up to date on the latest innovations.

Frankie listened, murmuring encouragement to keep Tommi talking. She loved seeing her sister so clearly happy, deeply in love with Max, excited about the baby and the success of her restaurant.

Cornelia joined them at the tiled island and poured herbal tea into mugs, setting one in front of Frankie with several tablets.

"Thanks, Mom." Frankie spooned honey into her tea.

"Enough about me." Tommi lifted her mug to sip. "What's new with you, Frankie? I've hardly seen you over the last few weeks."

"I've been busy at work." Frankie met Cornelia and Tommi's gazes and decided to be blunt. She needed to vent, and who better than family to understand? "And I've been seeing a lot of Eli."

Tommi's eyes widened. "Eli Wolf? Justin's friend?"

Frankie nodded, taking a brownie off the plate in the center of the island. The chocolate square had sinfully decadent, rich fudge frosting.

She glanced up to see Cornelia and Tommi exchanging glances.

"You didn't tell her we were at the fundraiser with you and Harry, Mom?"

Cornelia shook her head. "No, I didn't. To be honest, Frankie, I thought you and Eli were just together on a casual date. Much as I like Eli, he doesn't appear to be someone you'd ever get serious about, despite his being handsome, very charming and undeniably interested in you."

"Why didn't you think I might be seriously drawn to Eli?" Surprised, Frankie stared at her mother.

"I suppose because the men you've dated in the past have been more intellectually oriented, less...physical than Eli."

Frankie's eyes narrowed as she considered her mother's words. "It's true I've spent more time with men who earn their living in white-collar jobs, and Eli's definitely a blue-collar guy. But one of the things I like about Eli is that he's not intimidated by my job, or my college degrees. In fact, the subject never even comes up. Actually," she added slowly, thoughtfully, "he challenges me, makes me laugh, and I never feel as if I'm marking time with him until I can do something more interesting." She swept Cornelia and Tommi with a glance that surely reflected her surprise. "I hadn't realized that until just now. It's probably irrelevant after what happened Saturday."

"Why?" Tommi asked.

"What happened?" Cornelia's question melded with Tommi's.

Frankie quickly gave them an abbreviated version, ending with the last words she'd yelled at Eli, telling him she didn't want to talk to him until he was ready to apologize.

When she finished, Cornelia set her mug down with a snap. "Men," she muttered. "They can be so stubborn."

"Exactly," Frankie said with an abrupt nod of agreement.

"I always thought Eli was smooth with women—at least that's his reputation," Tommi added when Frankie glared at her. "But he certainly screwed up with you." She pursed her lips, her gaze considering. "I wonder why?"

"Because he's impossible, that's why." Frankie took a bite of chocolate brownie. Her eyes closed in sheer bliss. "Mom, these are amazing."

"Thank you. It's a new recipe," Cornelia said, distracted from what were clearly deep thoughts.

"If Max had done something like that," Tommi continued, undeterred, "I'd suspect it was because he was scared silly and terrified I'd be hurt. Nothing seems to shake Max, but since he loves me, he'd freak out if I was in danger."

"But I wasn't in danger," Frankie pointed out. "And Eli doesn't love me—we've only been dating for a couple of weeks or so."

"Time doesn't necessarily matter—not if it's the right person," Cornelia put in.

"And Eli didn't know you weren't in any real danger," Tommi pointed out.

"Which is why he should have asked me!" Frankie declared, angry all over again at how unreasonable Eli had been. "If he'd asked, I would have explained Daisy is as docile as a lamb."

"I don't think men can wait if they believe someone they love is in danger," Tommi told her. "They automatically shift into protection mode and ask questions later."

Frankie looked at her mother. Cornelia nodded in confirmation.

"Tommi's right," Cornelia said. "At least, that's been my observation. Even Harry, although he went about it in his usual bumbling way, tried very hard to protect all of us after your father died. If I'd allowed it, Harry would have wrapped us all in cotton wool, installed us in his mansion and hired nannies to care for you girls and a maid to wait on me."

"Yes, but that's Uncle Harry," Frankie pointed out reasonably. "He tends to bulldoze his way through life, unaware he's making people who love him crazy."

Cornelia rolled her eyes. "I can't deny that's a perfect description of Harry."

"You must have been a very determined woman to stand up to him all those years when we were growing up," Frankie told her.

Tommi laughed, amusement gleaming in her eyes. "That's an understatement. Uncle Harry still hasn't stopped trying to arrange our lives—look what he did with Bobbie and me."

"True." Frankie wished she could tell them Harry had set his sights on her. She'd love to confide the details of her and Eli's plan to thwart Harry's matchmaking scheme and get their perspective. "I wish he'd turn his attention elsewhere."

"So do I." Cornelia's mouth firmed, her eyes snapping militantly. "I'm getting tired of dealing with him—and being his last-minute date for functions. In fact, the golf pro at the club asked me out, and I said yes. Maybe Harry will stop taking us all for granted if we're not so available whenever he calls."

"Mom!" Frankie was speechless and suspected her shock was written on her face. She glanced at Tommi to see the same stunned surprise on her sister's face. "I've never heard you complain about Uncle Harry before."

"Well, you're hearing it now," Cornelia's cheeks pinkened, her eyes bright with annoyance beneath the smooth sleek chignon that swept her blond hair up and away from her face, exposing the clean lines of beautiful bone structure. "I've dealt with Harry for years, and frankly, I'm fed up."

Frankie couldn't imagine her mother staying angry at Harry. Cornelia had argued with Harry over the years, most often when he'd wanted to lavish her daughters with extravagant gifts. But the two had been friends since they were children.

Much as she wanted Harry to stop trying to fix her up with eligible men, she didn't want to see friction between him and her mother.

And Cornelia sounded as if she were upset with Harry on a personal level.

Surely Cornelia would soon calm, forgive Harry, and things would go on as usual. Wouldn't they?

Sharing tea, chatting and laughing with her mother and Tommi was just what she'd needed, Frankie reflected later as she drove home.

The phone rang just as she unlocked her condo door and she hurried inside, relocking the door behind her before walking quickly across the living room. She dropped her car keys and purse on the sofa and picked up the phone. "Hello?"

"Hi, Frankie, this is Harry."

Her anticipation deflated and she realized she'd hoped the caller was Eli.

"Hi, Uncle Harry." Phone tucked between shoulder and ear, she shrugged out of her coat and went to hang it up. "What are you up to?" she asked, curious.

"I've been working on a new software program that has the potential to revolutionize the future of robotics. But that's not why I called," he said abruptly. "I want to ask you about something, but I don't want you to tell your mother."

Frankie's eyebrows lifted. "All right. Unless it's something I think she needs to know about," she added hastily. This was, after all, Harry Hunt. Who knew what he was up to?

"Your mother told me the other night that she couldn't go to a function with me because she already had a date. I want to know who she's seeing."

His blunt request for information left Frankie speechless.

"Harry, I think you should ask Mom this question. If she wants you to know, she'll tell you."

"I can't ask Cornelia," Harry said impatiently. "She'd probably tell me to go take a flying leap."

Yes, she very well might, Frankie thought with a grin. "Nevertheless, I'm a little uncomfortable answering you, Uncle Harry, especially if you think Mom wouldn't want you to know."

"I didn't say I thought she doesn't want me to know," Harry growled. "I just said she'd make me suffer before she told me."

She couldn't hold back the laugh that bubbled up. "And you'd rather skip the suffering and just get the information?"

"Of course. Who wouldn't?" Harry sounded put out. "I can't believe Cornelia is dating someone else. Why would she do that?"

Frankie rolled her eyes. "Why wouldn't she, Uncle

Harry? She's an attractive, single woman. Why shouldn't she enjoy an active social life?"

"Because up until now, her social life has included me and apparently she's decided to change the rules, that's why." Harry's deep voice roared over the line.

Frankie winced and held the phone away from her ear.

"I'm sorry I yelled," he said immediately, frustration apparent in his voice. "But I don't understand why you're reluctant to tell me what I need to know."

"All right." Frankie made a swift decision. "Mom's been dating the golf pro at her club."

"Greg?" Harry's voice was incredulous. "He's too young for her."

"I suspect the same could be said about the women you've dated in the past," Frankie told him evenly. "And I don't see why Mom shouldn't go out with Greg if she wants. I think she's having fun."

"Fun." Harry's voice was totally without expression.

"Yes, fun," Frankie said firmly. "I wouldn't be surprised if their relationship develops into something deeper," she added thoughtfully. "He's very nice to her."

"He's nice to her." Again, Harry repeated her words with no inflection whatsoever.

"Very nice," Frankie said.

"Well…" Silence spun out. "Thanks," he said abruptly. And he hung up.

Frankie shook her head, exasperated. Sometimes,

Harry took abruptness to a whole new level, she thought as she headed for the shower.

The brief conversation had distracted her and lifted her spirits, but thoughts of Eli intruded as Frankie showered and dressed in comfortable flannel pajama bottoms and a cotton knit top.

She refused to keep thinking about him, however, and managed to stay busy, writing copy for the volunteers' section of the horse barn's website, until bedtime.

Once she fell asleep, however, she couldn't force thoughts of Eli to the back of her mind and he returned full force, featuring prominently in dreams filled with arguments that ended with the two of them in bed.

Chapter Eleven

Late Sunday afternoon brought a respite from the downpour of rain with weak sunshine that continued through Monday. But by Tuesday, another winter storm had blown in off the Pacific, bringing with it more rain and dark skies.

Eli sent the work crew home early, and by five-thirty he'd showered, donned dry clothes and driven to Justin's house for dinner. Ava was in the kitchen with Lily, happily tearing up lettuce for salad and "helping" her mother with other cooking chores. Eli joined Justin in the game room, where they relaxed with a friendly game of pool.

"What's going on with you and Frankie?"

"What do you mean?" Bent over the pool table, cue in hand, Eli didn't need to look at Justin to know his friend's expression was as casual as his voice. He also knew Justin's question wasn't the slightest bit casual.

"Dad tells me you two are dating."

"We've been out a few times," Eli conceded. He tapped the four ball into a side pocket and stood to walk around the table, considering his next shot.

"Lily says Cornelia saw you two kissing at a fundraiser."

"Did she?"

"Apparently, Cornelia said it wasn't just a friendly kiss on the cheek."

"Hmm." Eli grunted a noncommittal reply and bent over to line up his cue stick.

"And since you're refusing to talk about her," Justin went on, his voice mild, "I can only assume you're trying to seduce my cousin."

Eli jerked upright. "I am *not* trying to seduce Frankie," he ground out. Justin smiled and lifted an eyebrow. "Oh, hell." Eli tossed the cue stick onto the table, scattering the remaining balls, and stalked to the sideboard. He poured himself a shot of whiskey and downed it, scowling at Justin. "And I'm not sleeping with her, if that's what you're asking."

"Are you saying you don't want to?"

"Hell, no!" Eli thrust his fingers through his hair and slammed the shot glass down on the glossy mahogany bar. "She's a beautiful woman. Any sane man would want to sleep with her. But I'm not." He glared at Justin.

Justin leaned his cue against the wall and joined Eli

at the bar. He took a bottle of imported beer from the refrigerator concealed behind a mahogany panel and pried off the cap with an opener.

"But you'd like to," Justin nudged, tipping the bottle to drink.

"That's a helluva question for you to be asking about your favorite cousin," Eli growled.

"Not really." Justin shrugged. "Frankie's a grown woman. She's smart, able to make her own choices."

"If you think that, then why are you asking me about her?" Eli said.

"Because ever since her last birthday, I've noticed you watching her when you thought she wasn't looking."

"So?" Eli spun the empty shot glass on the bar, turning it in slow circles.

"So I recognize the look in your eyes. Damned if you don't remind me of myself, before Lily agreed to marry me."

Eli's head lifted, his eyes narrowing over Justin's half smile. "What the hell does that mean?"

"It means, friend, that I think my pretty cousin has you tagged and bagged."

Eli snorted. "In your dreams. This isn't hunting season, and I'm not somebody's trophy."

"No, you're not." Justin smiled and shook his head. "I remember fighting the inevitable myself, for as long as I could. But looking back, I wish I hadn't wasted so much time—I could have been with Lily and Ava from the beginning."

Eli stared at his friend. He remembered too well how

grim Justin had been during those months when he'd been separated from Lily. He also remembered telling Justin he was a bloody idiot after he'd confessed he'd left the woman he loved because he'd been convinced he couldn't be a good husband—or father.

"Me and Frankie—our situation isn't anything like yours with Lily," he growled finally.

"Not the little details," Justin conceded. "But for a guy, the core reason women like Lily and Frankie scare us to death is because we know they could clip our wings for good." Justin retrieved his pool cue and strolled to the table. "Men are hunters—we don't settle down easily."

Eli knew having Frankie in his life permanently had been figuring prominently in his dreams lately. So he only grunted noncommittally and picked up his own cue off the green felt tabletop. He took a seat on one of the tall stools at the old-fashioned bar and observed as Justin walked around the table, gauging potential shots with a critical eye.

"You seem happy enough," he said.

Justin glanced up. "I am." He leaned forward, lined up the shot and tapped the six ball into a side pocket. He rose, gave a faint grunt of satisfaction and chalked the end of his cue. "Lily's the best thing that ever happened to me. And Ava." He smiled fondly. "She's the icing on the cake."

"Think you'll have more kids?" Eli asked idly.

"We both would like at least one more." Justin set down the chalk on the edge of the table and eyed the position of the seven ball. "But the timing's up to Lily—she's got a lot on her plate right now at work."

"Do you ever worry about her?"

Justin looked up, frowning. "Worry? In what way?"

Eli shrugged. "Her safety—does she do things that scare the hell out of you?"

Justin squinted, considering the question. "Not so far—but she's pretty independent, so I wouldn't be surprised if she might, someday. Why?"

"Just wondering."

"What did Frankie do?" Justin asked with shrewd insight.

"Tried to push a horse several dozen times her weight into a barn stall." Just thinking about it made Eli scowl.

"You were up at the horse barn with Frankie?" Justin sounded surprised.

"Not with her, exactly. I drove up to Arlington to surprise her when I came home early from Vegas. Scared the hell out of me when I saw her with that mountain of a horse."

Justin let his pool cue slide through his fingers until it hit the floor, butt-end first. "And what did you do?" he asked.

"Same thing any guy would do—I moved her out of the way and put the horse in the stall."

Justin stared at him for a long, silent moment. "And what did she do?"

"She yelled at me." Eli thrust his fingers through his

hair. "Told me I was being an ass. That was right before she told me she didn't want to talk to me again."

"Damn, Eli, that's harsh."

"Tell me about it," he growled. "All I was doing was making sure she was safe. You should have seen the size of that horse—it was huge."

"I'm guessing Frankie didn't see it your way." Justin's smile was wry. "She's been volunteering at that stable since she was a kid, probably worked with that particular horse more than once."

"That's what I got from what she said," Eli admitted. "Which I didn't realize when I caught sight of her with that huge mare."

"Would it have made a difference?" Justin asked.

"Probably not," Eli admitted. "I acted on instinct."

"Something Frankie's not likely to accept as an excuse," Justin told him. "She's pretty independent."

"No kidding," Eli muttered.

"Frankie's usually willing to listen to a reasonable argument, though," Justin said. "Have you explained to her why you did what you did?"

"No. I sent her flowers, but I haven't talked to her."

"Did you at least put a note in the flowers saying you're sorry?"

"No," Eli growled. "Because I'm damned sure I'd do it all over again, given the circumstances."

Justin grinned, white teeth flashing in his tanned face. "You've got it bad, Eli. You're in love."

"I'm not in love," Eli said stubbornly. "Just because I

worry that she might get hurt doesn't mean I'm in love with her."

Justin shrugged and laughed out loud. "Have it your way, but it sure sounds like love to me."

His cell phone rang before Eli could reply. Justin took the silver phone from his pocket and flipped it open, glancing at the number before answering.

"Hey, Frankie, what's up?"

Eli stiffened, going more tense as Justin's grin was quickly replaced with a frown.

"No problem. I'll have Lily put dinner on hold and be right there. Wait in the car, I won't be long." He listened a moment. "Don't worry about it. Sit tight and I'll be there in about fifteen minutes."

"What's wrong?" Eli demanded when Justin shoved the phone back in his pocket.

"Frankie worked late, and when she went out to the parking lot to go home, her car wouldn't start."

"I'll go." Eli slid his pool cue back into the wall cabinet and turned to the door.

"Are you sure? I thought you weren't talking to her."

Eli flicked his friend a glance over his shoulder. "You take care of Lily. I'll make sure Frankie's okay."

Justin's chuckle of amusement followed Eli down the hall as he collected his coat and left the house.

Frankie tucked her chin into the collar of her coat and crossed her arms over her chest. The temperature outside her car was hovering around forty degrees, but the damp air and cold rain pounding her windshield made it feel colder. The university parking lot was nearly empty, with only a few vehicles spaced around the big tarmac area.

She wished she hadn't picked tonight to work late. Or that her car hadn't chosen tonight to stop running. If she'd left her office at the usual time, she could have caught a ride home with a friend and called the repair garage from the warmth of her condo.

Sighing, she pulled her purse nearer and searched through it for a granola bar. Then she remembered she'd eaten it at lunch. Her stomach growled, and she pressed her palm against her abdomen.

Working late after eating only a granola bar and a container of yogurt for lunch hadn't been a wise choice, she thought wryly.

The only sound was the rain, hammering on the metal roof of her car. Frankie had a swift, mental image of being curled up with Eli on her sofa while the rain pounded down outside the windows.

Stop thinking about Eli, she ordered herself.

She still didn't know what to do about him. Tommi's observation that Eli had reacted the same way her Max would have had made Frankie wonder if there was any possibility Eli felt more than lust for her.

While she was vacillating, unable to make up her mind, she'd arrived home Monday to find a bouquet of bright spring flowers in front of her door. The card had only the initial *E,* the black script decisive and dark. She knew instantly it was from Eli.

She loved the flowers, and something about the gesture eased the faint ache in her heart. But he hadn't called, and three days had passed. She'd started to wonder if the flowers were his way of saying goodbye.

A vehicle turned into the parking lot and drew nearer, the headlights arcing over her car as the truck pulled up and parked next to her. Frankie had expected Justin's Porsche, but it took only a second of confusion before she recognized the driver.

What on earth is Eli doing here? she thought as her heart beat faster.

He stepped out of the truck, hunching his shoulders against the rain as he jogged to her car and tapped on the window. Frankie rolled the glass down, just far enough to talk to him. Even that small opening let wind-blown rain inside.

"Hi." She was so glad to see him she could have hugged him. "Where's Justin?"

"He's home having dinner. Let's get you in my truck. You might as well stay warm while I check out your car."

She nodded and pushed open the door. Eli pulled open the passenger door of his truck, and before she could climb in, he caught her around the waist and lifted her onto the high seat. Frankie caught her breath. Even through the layers of raincoat and the cashmere sweater she wore beneath, his touch made her breathing falter.

"Thanks," she murmured as he tucked her coat hem inside.

"No problem. Turn up the heater if you're cold. I'll only be a minute."

The interior of the truck cab was wonderfully warm. Frankie stretched out her legs to let the air from the heater vent warm her cold toes. Through the rain-streaked truck window, she could see Eli as he raised the hood of her car and fiddled with something on the engine.

Then he slid behind the wheel. She thought he turned the key but couldn't see clearly before he exited, slammed the hood down, and jogged around the truck. When he opened the door and slid behind the wheel, he brought the scent of rain and fresh air with him.

"Did you fix it?" she asked.

"No. I think the battery's dead." He shifted the truck into gear, and they left the parking lot. "I'll take you home and come back in the morning with jumper cables. I usually carry a set in the truck, but Matt borrowed them last week and didn't return them." His deep voice was reserved, carefully polite.

She hesitated a moment. "I can't thank you enough for doing this, Eli. I hope you know how much I appreciate it."

"No problem." He flicked a hooded glance over to her before looking out the windshield again. "Have you had dinner?"

"No. But I'm sure there's something at home in the fridge I can warm up." She eyed him with curiosity. "How did you happen to get stuck rescuing me in the rain?"

"Justin and I were playing pool at his house when he talked to you. I volunteered to come get you."

"I see." Frankie wanted to ask him why he'd offered to come out in the downpour to help her, especially since the last time she'd seen him, she'd told him she didn't want to talk to him.

They stopped at a red light. Eli picked up his cell phone from the seat divider, dialing from memory. While they waited for the light to turn green, he placed an order for take-out Thai food.

"You missed dinner with Justin and Lily in order to come get me, didn't you?" she asked as the traffic light changed from amber to green and Eli accelerated down the street.

He shrugged. "I'll see them next week—Justin's barbecuing steaks for Granddad on Saturday."

"Nevertheless, I'm sorry you had to miss dinner tonight because of me."

"Trust me, it's not a problem." He glanced sideways, a brief smile curving his mouth. "I can have dinner at Justin's anytime. Rescuing a pretty woman is more important—especially if she'll agree to share Thai take-out with me."

His smile eased the uncomfortable, faintly unsettled tension in Frankie, and she smiled back at him. "I have a bottle of wine that would be perfect with Thai food."

"Sounds good."

Eli braked, slotting the truck into an empty space in front of a Thai restaurant at the foot of Queen Anne.

"I'll be right back." He left the truck's engine running,

the heater continuing to blow warm air on Frankie's damp feet. The windshield wipers swished rhythmically as he jogged through the rain and disappeared inside the restaurant. Moments later, he returned. The two brown bags he tucked behind the seat filled the cab's interior with mouthwatering smells.

"What kept you at work so late?" he asked as he pulled out of the parking slot and headed for her condo building.

"A department staff meeting," she told him. "Even though I'm subbing in English Lit, I'm still technically a part of the research department. In order to stay involved with decisions on future projects, I have to attend staff meetings."

"Isn't it unusual to have someone in research lecturing in the classroom?" Eli asked, curious.

"I suppose it is," she replied. "But the circumstances were unique. The English department needed someone immediately, and not only was I temporarily unassigned, since I'd just completed a project, but I have a doctorate in English Lit and I'm qualified to teach." She shrugged. "It was an easy fix."

"Do you enjoy the change?" He glanced sideways at her. "Or are you counting the days until you're back on your regular schedule?"

"I'm enjoying it," she told him with a smile. "But then, I love my job in research, too."

"When will you go back to it—next quarter?"

"I'm not sure. The return date for the professor on emergency leave is open-ended."

A few moments of silence passed until they reached Frankie's building. Eli parked and got out, jogging around the truck to open her door; together, they ran through the rain to the lobby.

Inside Frankie's condo, she slipped out of her raincoat and tugged off her boots.

"You can leave your wet things here," she told Eli as she picked up her purse and briefcase. She dropped them on the seat cushion of an armchair as she passed it on her way into the kitchen.

He shrugged out of his jacket and pulled off his boots before following her. "Where's the bottle of wine?"

"In the cabinet below the coffeemaker." She lifted plates down from an upper cupboard while Eli set the bags of Thai takeout on the table and located the wine.

Frankie went up on tiptoe to reach stemmed wine glasses on a higher shelf, but they were just barely beyond her fingertips.

"Here, let me." Eli stretched above her, his chest pressing against her back as he easily lifted two glasses and set them on the countertop.

His body radiated heat; she felt it from her shoulders to her knees, his chest lightly touching her back, his thighs barely brushing hers. Her eyes closed, and she drew in a deep breath.

Eli stilled. Then his palms settled on the countertop on each side of her, his big body bracketing hers. His head bent, and she felt him brush his face against her hair.

"Frankie," his deep voice murmured in her ear. "I'm sorry I upset you the other day at the barn. I didn't mean to insult your intelligence. I saw you with a horse as big as a mountain and instinct took over. I only wanted to protect you."

Frankie turned, looking up into his face as she searched his eyes. She found only sincerity.

"I'd like to swear I'd never do that again, but I can't lie to you." His face hardened. "If I thought you were in danger, I'd probably act on instinct and try to protect you."

Any remaining anger leached away, receding behind a warm swell of emotion and leaving Frankie amused at his expression. Eli was braced, clearly expecting her to be angry at him.

"As far as apologies go, that's just about the worst one I've ever heard," she told him, sliding her hands up the fine wool sleeves covering his forearms, over the swell of biceps under his black V-neck sweater, until her fingers curled over the slope of his shoulders. "You're sorry but you'd do it again?" She laughed at the chagrined look on his face. "Couldn't you have stopped at 'I'm sorry'?"

"I should have," he agreed, the taut line of his mouth easing into a slow, sexy grin. "But I didn't think lying was a good plan."

"Will you at least promise to ask me if I know what I'm doing the next time, and if I want or need help before you barge in and save me?" she asked, enjoying the sense of leashed power beneath her fingers and palms.

"I promise I'll try." He bent his head, resting his forehead against hers. "You scared the hell out of me, Frankie. Compared to the size of that horse, you're tiny."

"I suppose I am," she conceded. "And since you hadn't seen Daisy before, you had no way of knowing she's as harmless as a friendly puppy. But still…" She eyed him, wanting to make her point. "You need to ask me next time."

A frown drew his dark brows down, and he leaned back to search her features. "Just for the record—are you doing anything else dangerous on a regular basis?"

"Oh, no." Frankie smiled up at him, laughing aloud when relief erased the worry lines. She lifted on her toes, pressing an impulsive, affectionate kiss on his mouth.

Eli immediately caught her close, taking over as he ravaged her mouth with a possessive, claiming kiss. When he lowered her back on her heels, she was breathless.

"Maybe we should eat," he suggested, deep voice rasping.

"Yes," she said, her own voice husky with arousal. "That's a great idea."

"In here at the table—or in the living room?" he asked.

"Living room, I think. We can turn on the news or a movie."

"Sounds good." Eli poured wine into the glasses and carried them into the living room, returning to carry off the plates, utensils and napkins as Frankie set them on the counter.

Frankie joined him with the two take-out bags, which she immediately unloaded onto the low coffee table. Eli opened the first few white boxes, and the aroma of spicy food reminded them both that they were ravenous.

"That was delicious," Frankie said after emptying her plate. She curled her feet under her and settled back on the sofa, a glass of wine cradled in her hands.

Eli set his glass on the coffee table and, in one easy move, tugged her feet across the sofa cushion and propped them on his thigh. Startled, Frankie was about to protest when he ran his thumb down the arch of her right foot and pressed.

"Ohh," she groaned, half closing her eyes. "That feels so wonderful."

"Good."

She lifted her lashes to find him watching her, a slow smile curving his mouth, his eyes that smoky, darker blue she loved.

He shrugged, his hands continuing to massage her foot. "Just part of my attempt to seduce you, ma'am," he drawled.

She laughed. "Where did you get the cowboy accent?" she asked.

"It's part of the seduction," he told her. "Women love cowboys, don't they?"

"Let me think. Except for Justin, the only cowboys

I've seen are ones in the movies. Definitely a lot to love there, so, yes, I suppose women do love cowboys."

"See? The cowboy vibe works. That's where the 'ma'am' came from." He winked at her. "Throw in foot massage, Thai food and flowers and a guy has a chance with a lady."

Frankie rolled her eyes in disbelief. "Does this line actually work with the women you date?"

"Sometimes." He shrugged. "Sometimes they just say thank you for the foot rub and tell me to go home." He picked up her other foot and rubbed her arch.

She nearly groaned aloud again. "I won't tell you to go home," she murmured.

He shot her a look from beneath his lashes, his eyes flashing blue. "Does that mean I can stay the night?"

Frankie knew the seemingly casual question was anything but—Eli had made no secret that he wanted her. She loved his bluntness because it freed her from the usual games men played. Was she ready to sleep with him? She wanted him, but the wariness that demanded she protect her heart still told her to wait. She wasn't sure what she was waiting for, exactly. She'd long since moved past believing she was seeing Eli only as part of a scheme to distract Harry. And she knew her love of independence was fast taking second place to the sheer pleasure of sharing time with Eli. But Frankie believed in listening to her instincts and those instincts were whispering wait. Reluctantly, she heeded the warning.

"I don't think so," she said. "Not yet."

"At least you didn't say never," he told her with a wry

grin. "I'll just have to keep trying." He lifted her bare feet from his thigh and set them on the cushion. "We need music," he declared, pushing to his feet.

"Why?" Taken by surprise, she looked up at him.

"Because dancing is the next item on the seduction list," he told her, his gaze flicking over the room, stopping on the radio and CD player on the shelf below the television set. He knelt on one knee to switch off the audio on the TV and turn on the radio. Instantly, the room was filled with a slow, bluesy tune from Seattle's jazz station.

"Nice music." He rose and walked to the sofa. "Dance with me, Frankie."

Lifting the glass from her hand, he set it on the table and caught her fingers in his to draw her up from the soft cushions.

He tucked her close with his hands at her waist, and she wrapped her arms around his neck, her fingers testing the silky black hair at his nape as his arms hugged her closer. They moved slowly in time to the music, bodies swaying in the lamplit room.

Eli's arms tightened, his hands smoothing over the soft strip of bare skin in the space between the hem of her sweater and the waistband of her skirt.

"Should I worry about losing my head and being seduced?" Frankie murmured against his throat.

She felt his lips curve against her temple. "Not unless you want to be. Of course," he drawled, his powerful thighs moving against hers as they swayed to the music, "any time you want to lure me into your bed, feel free.

I'm just a poor innocent country boy, so you could probably have your way with me before I knew what you were up to."

Frankie tilted her head back, laughing as she met his gaze. "You're an innocent country boy? Is this part of the cowboy-vibe thing?"

"Yup. Be gentle with me."

Frankie was laughing when he kissed her. His warm lips curved in a smile as they settled over hers.

"I missed you," she sighed when his head lifted and she tucked her face against the strong, warm column of his throat. Each breath she took drew in the subtle tang of his aftershave and, beneath it, the elusive male scent she'd come to associate with Eli. "Let's not fight anymore."

His arms tightened reflexively, pressing her closer.

"No," he rasped in agreement. "Let's not fight."

Their bodies moved together, the very air thickening with heat.

"I missed you, too."

Frankie's heart slammed in her throat. "Did you?" she whispered.

He nodded, his cheek, faintly rough with beard stubble, moving against her hair. "Too much." His voice was deeper, rougher. He stopped dancing, his mouth claiming hers with unmistakable desire.

Chapter Twelve

Frankie felt surrounded by Eli as he swung her off her feet and carried her to the sofa. His much bigger frame crowded hers on the wide cushions, but Frankie didn't care. She was swept up in the heat that exploded between them.

This was what she'd always wanted, needed, and had never found in any man she'd dated before. The passion that roared out of control between them was irresistible, and Frankie didn't try to fight it. Confident in his willingness to stop if she said no, she let desire pull her under, reveling in the shudder that shook his big frame when she slid her hands under his sweater and stroked her palms up the length of his bare back.

Eli tugged at her sweater, his hand flattening over the bare skin of her ribcage above her waistband.

When his fingers brushed over the soft swell of her breast above her bra, Frankie murmured against his mouth, shifting beneath the heavy thigh covering her own.

Long heated moments passed before Eli gradually eased them back from the edge, his kisses soothing rather than stoking the fire between them. At last, he lifted his head and looked down at her.

"Honey, if you're not going to ask me to stay for breakfast, we'd better go back to watching TV."

Dazed, Frankie stared up at him, struggling to process the switch from passion to practicality.

"I…"

The phone rang, startling both of them.

"Do you need to answer that?" Eli asked.

"I suppose I should."

He lifted away from her, stretched across the sofa and grabbed the phone from the end table and handed it to her. Frankie sat upright and slid her feet to the floor.

"Hello?" She frowned slightly. "Yes, this is Frankie Fairchild." Her eyes widened. "Oh, hello, Nicholas. How nice to hear from you."

Beside her, Eli's big body tensed. She glanced at him to find him watching her, eyes narrowed, his face inscrutable.

She paused, listening. "Much as I'd love to, I'm afraid I'm busy on Saturday. I'm so sorry."

Frankie exchanged a few more polite comments with Nicholas, then rushed to end the call, clearly impatient—and mad. "I'm so sorry, Nicholas, but my date just arrived. I'm afraid I have to ring off—lovely to hear from you. Yes, I'll tell Mom hello for you. Bye."

She switched the phone off and looked at Eli.

"That was Nicholas Dean," she said unnecessarily. "He told me he ran into Harry and Mom this afternoon and they mentioned how much I've been wanting to see the new musical at the Pantages. And since he has tickets, he thought we could go together."

"I bet he did," Eli said, his voice a growl.

"Harry's still matchmaking—and with Nicholas." Frankie could hardly believe it. "He *knows* you and I have been dating. And so does Mom. Why on earth would she have gone along with Harry nudging Nicholas to ask me out?"

"I don't know. I thought she liked me," Eli commented, a muscle flexing along his jawline. He stood, raking his hair back. "Maybe she likes the idea of you paired with Nicholas better."

"Oh, no, Eli. I'm sure that's not true." Frankie rose to slide her arms around his waist, and Eli instantly slipped his arms around her, tugging her forward until she rested against his hard length. "It's far more likely that Harry was not so subtly encouraging Nicholas to call me and Mom wasn't able to stop him. You know how Harry is when he gets an idea fixed in his head— he's like a bulldozer with no brakes."

"That's true." Eli nodded, his hands smoothing over her waist. "And apparently he's still fixated on getting you and Nicholas together." He looked down at her. "You're sure you're not interested in him?"

She shook her head.

"Thank God." He narrowed his eyes over her. "I've always liked Nicholas, but I'm not sure we'd stay friends if you went out with him."

"Are you saying you might be unfriendly if you ran into him?" Frankie asked.

"I'm saying I'm not normally a violent man, but I'm making no promises if you start dating other men."

"Just so we're clear," she said slowly, suppressing a smile. "Are you saying you want us to be exclusive and not date other people?"

"That's exactly what I'm saying, and you know it," he told her, eyes gleaming with amusement.

"I just wanted to be clear. And to be even more clear, you're asking me, not telling me, correct?"

He nodded. "Absolutely. I would never order an intelligent, independent woman such as yourself not to date other men. I'm sure you'd call me a neanderthal if I did."

"Yes," she told him primly. "I certainly would."

"Then I can count myself lucky we're in agreement." He picked her up, her feet dangling in the air, and kissed her.

The kiss was hot, carnal and a fierce declaration of possession, branding Frankie as surely as if he'd marked her. When he lowered her feet to the floor, she had to clutch his arms to keep from staggering.

"Since you won't let me stay for breakfast, I think it's time for me to leave, while I can still tear myself away."

Much to her satisfaction, Eli's breathing was as ragged as hers.

He wrapped an arm around her shoulders, and they walked to the door.

Moments later, after he'd donned jacket and boots and they'd shared another kiss that left her feeling dazed and hot, he left.

As Frankie turned out her bedside lamp later, she vowed to have a talk with Harry and her mother. She was certain Cornelia must have been an innocent bystander to Harry's machinations.

But Harry better be prepared to explain why he's continuing to interfere in my love life when it's clear Eli and I are involved, she thought with determination.

Frankie called Cornelia the following morning and, after chatting for a few moments, learned her mother was meeting Harry at his house that evening after work.

"Why don't you join us, Frankie?" Cornelia said. "We're going over the applications for the HuntCom college scholarship program. I'd love to have your input, and I know Harry would, too."

"What time?" Frankie asked, listening as Cornelia gave her the details. When she hung up, she'd promised to join them for an hour.

And she planned to use most of that hour grilling Harry about his matchmaking efforts, she thought with determination.

When she pulled into Harry's driveway that evening, Cornelia's Volvo was parked next to a long, black town car. Frankie slotted her BMW in beside the limo and walked quickly down the walk. She glanced at the sky over the lake, thankful that the Pacific Northwest was enjoying a beautiful clear day although the sun was already low on the horizon, sinking behind the Seattle skyline.

"Good evening, Sonja," she said as Harry's longtime maid opened the door. "I'm meeting my mother here—is she in the library with Harry?"

"Yes, miss." Sonja took her coat. "Will you be staying for dinner?"

Frankie shook her head. "I doubt it, not tonight."

In fact, she thought as she left the maid and walked through the house to reach the library, she might not be staying more than a few minutes. It all depended on whether Harry agreed to cease his attempts to fix her up with Nicholas Dean.

She'd long since grown accustomed to the opulent home Harry had built with the fortune he'd made from HuntCom, the computer software corporation he'd built through sheer genius and hard work. Cornelia and her husband had grown up with Harry; the two men had been partners when HuntCom was a fledgling firm operated out of Harry's garage. When Frankie's father died suddenly, leaving little money for his widow and daughters, Harry had tried to convince Cornelia to let him take care of her and the girls. But Cornelia had refused, stubbornly determined to make her own way. She'd sold their big house and moved her daughters back to her family home in Queen Anne, then taken a job working at a private school to fund their education. Through sheer determination and shrewd acumen, Cornelia had managed to raise her girls with only minimal ·interference from Harry. She'd accepted his offer of educational traveling during school vacations, however, and reluctantly agreed when he gave them each a large sum of money upon high school graduation.

Frankie had used Harry's graduation gift to pay her tuition while she earned two master's degrees and a PhD.

Much as she adored her uncle Harry, however, she was determined to take a firm stand on the issue of his matchmaking. He'd simply stepped beyond what any self-respecting woman could accept, she thought as she entered the library.

"There you are, Frankie," Cornelia greeted her with a welcoming smile. She and Harry were seated at a cherrywood library table halfway down the long room.

At the far end of the room, facing a wall of windows and French doors that led to a patio, was Harry's massive mahogany desk. The room provided a fabulous view of Lake Washington and the Seattle skyline beyond.

Frankie's heels tapped on the polished wooden floors, grew muffled as she crossed a deep-piled oriental carpet, then clicked on bare flooring once more.

"Hello, Mom, Harry." Frankie set her purse on the table and took the chair on Harry's right. He sat at the end of the table, Cornelia on his left, several stacks of papers arranged on the glossy surface. Both he and Cornelia had sheets of paper and a small group of scholarship applications on the table in front of them. A coffee-service tray took up space just beyond Cornelia.

"I'm so glad you could make it," Cornelia said. "I'd love your input on several of the applications. We've narrowed down the number, as you can see." She gestured at the smaller stacks.

"I'm happy to help, Mom," Frankie replied, her back ramrod straight and several inches away from the back of her chair. "But first, I need to talk to you and Harry."

"Oh?" Cornelia glanced from her to Harry, a puzzled frown pleating her brow. "What about?"

"I had a phone call last night—from Nicholas Dean."

The brief flash of guilt that flickered across Harry's features confirmed Frankie's suspicions that he'd instigated the call.

"Uncle Harry, I specifically told you the night we were all here for dinner that I wasn't interested in Nicholas," she told him. "And yet you're apparently trying to push the two of us together."

"Harry!" Cornelia's expression was appalled, her dismay echoed in her voice. "Please tell me you haven't been meddling in Frankie's love life."

"Now, just a minute," Harry blustered, his cheeks flushed. "I wouldn't call it meddling."

"What *would* you call it?" Frankie demanded.

"Well," he grumbled. "I only mentioned that you'd been wanting to see the new musical at the Pantages, that's all."

"And?" Frankie prompted when he paused.

"All right," he admitted. "I might have suggested Nicholas should phone you."

Frankie groaned. "Why do you keep doing this?" she asked, genuinely perplexed. "First with your own sons, then with Tommi and Bobbie—and now me! You've got to stop interfering in our lives."

"My sons are all happily married, and Tommi and Bobbie appear very happy, so how is that a bad thing?" Harry asked.

"You were lucky, Uncle Harry—what if your sons or my sisters had ended up brokenhearted, or divorced?"

"But they didn't," he insisted with stubborn logic.

"But you couldn't have known how things would turn out when you started throwing people together," Frankie pointed out. "And it could have been a disaster."

"I only wanted you and your sisters to be as happy as my boys," Harry said. "Even your mother thought Nicholas was right for you."

Frankie's eyes widened. "Mom, please tell me you didn't know Harry was doing this. I assumed you were an innocent bystander when Harry cornered Nicholas and told him to phone me." The sense of betrayal was sharp. Surely her mother wouldn't have gone along with Harry's crazy scheme?

"I had nothing to do with that," Cornelia said firmly. She frowned at Harry, her eyes accusing. "I admit we discussed how much we liked Nicholas the night of the Children's Hospital fundraiser. I may even have commented that he seemed more of a match for you than

Eli, but I *never* told Harry to interfere and set you up with Nicholas."

"Of course she didn't," Harry put in abruptly. "But there's no ignoring the facts. You're twenty-nine, Frankie. You need to marry soon—or you'll miss your best childbearing years."

"My best childbearing years?" Frankie seethed. "You make it sound as if I'm a brood mare, Harry."

"No, no, that's not what I meant," he said quickly, looking harried. "I only meant having younger people in my life as I get older—my sons, you and your sisters, my granddaughter, Ava—is one of the greatest joys I know. But I wasn't aware it would be so when I was your age." He gestured at Cornelia. "And your mother would make a wonderful grandmother, not to mention how much she'd love having grandchildren."

"Harry." Cornelia was clearly restraining herself. "I have the urge to rap you over the head with my umbrella. How on earth can you be so dense about people?"

Harry looked bewildered. "I only wanted you to know the joy of having little ones in the family again, Cornelia. At our age, it's a wonderful thing." His jaw firmed, and he straightened. "And you must admit, if Frankie continues as she has for the last several years, she'll probably have earned more university degrees by the time she's forty, but she won't have children."

"If you're suggesting that I'm too bookish to have sex, Uncle Harry," Frankie said with deadly calm, "then you don't know me at all." She pushed back her chair and stood. "Eli and I have been sleeping together for ages," she declared with dramatic flair. "And if hot, sweaty, amazingly fabulous sex is a guarantee of pregnancy, then I'm probably pregnant already." She was lying through her teeth, but Harry didn't know that, and her rashly impulsive claim was worth the guilt she might feel later, Frankie thought as Harry's eyes widened and his face grew even redder. She glanced at Cornelia and saw her mother's eyebrows raise with surprise. Much to her relief, she also saw a spark of amusement as Cornelia glanced at Harry and then back at Frankie.

Frankie picked up her purse. "I'm sorry I can't stay and help with the applications. Perhaps I can go over them later in the week at your house, Mom?"

"Of course, dear." Cornelia smiled benignly at her.

But as Frankie turned to leave, she saw her mother turn to face Harry, her expression threatening.

"Harry, explain yourself." Cornelia's demand held an ominous tone even Harry couldn't ignore, Frankie thought as she swept out of the library and then out of the house.

She hadn't wanted to confront Harry about his matchmaking, because she was well aware he had good intentions and meant well. But sometimes, she told herself as she drove home, there was no other recourse than to be blunt and forceful.

Which pretty much described how Cornelia was probably dealing with him at the moment, she thought with a grin.

* * *

"Harry Hunt, I cannot believe you're doing this again."

"Now, Cornelia, you know we discussed how much Frankie and Nicholas have in common," Harry said, trying to placate her. "And how great it would be if they got together."

"That doesn't mean I wanted you to blatantly suggest Nicholas should call and ask her out." Cornelia was livid, her eyes snapping with frustration. "For heaven's sake, Harry, how many times do you have to be told to stop interfering in our children's lives? First your sons—and that came much too close to being disastrous," she said. "And now my girls? You've got to stop this. No more!"

"My boys are all happily married," he pointed out in an attempt to reason with her. "And if I hadn't given them an ultimatum, God knows whether they ever would have considered marriage."

"We'll have to agree to disagree on the subject of your sons," Cornelia told him. "But as for my daughters…" She stood, picked up her purse, and pointed her index finger at him. "Leave my girls alone, Harry. Period."

And with that, Cornelia turned on her heel and marched regally out of the library, leaving Harry to mumble and mutter and stare morosely at the closed door.

He'd really angered Cornelia this time, he thought,

and Frankie, too. Much as he hated to give in, he supposed he'd have to abandon his efforts to get Frankie and Nicholas together.

Too bad, he mused. They had so much in common.

Harry frowned, thinking about Frankie's stunning declaration.

If Eli's sleeping with Frankie, Harry decided grimly, *he'd better have marriage in mind.*

I think I'll have a talk with him. Harry shoved away from the table and stood to stride out of the library, his steps purposeful.

Chapter Thirteen

Harry's black limo pulled into the Wolf Construction building site near the university campus late the following afternoon. The long car bumped and rolled over the rough dirt-and-gravel surface, its tires splashing through muddy puddles left from predawn showers.

The driver slotted the big car into an area in front of the work trailer. The pickups and cars of the work crew had long since left the lot, but Eli's work truck was still parked in front of the trailer. Harry exited the vehicle, his long, black overcoat flapping in the breeze as he climbed the wooden steps and knocked on the door. No one answered. He turned, scanning the scaffolding of the building under construction on his left.

"Harry," Eli called as he stepped between the studs

of a first-floor garage and strode across the lot toward him. "What brings you out here so late?"

"I was hoping to talk to you. Have you got a few minutes?"

"Sure. Let's go inside." Eli led the way into the portable office. "Have a seat, Harry. Want something to drink?" he asked over his shoulder as he took a mug off the pegs on the wall above the coffeemaker.

"I could use a cup of coffee, black," Harry replied, hands shoved in his coat pockets as he inspected the blueprints taped on the wall next to the drafting table.

"Here you are." Eli handed Harry a steaming mug and leaned his hips against the drafting table, muddy work boots crossed at the ankle. "So, what can I do for you, Harry?"

"Frankie came by the house last night," Harry said. "And after what she told her mother and me, I decided to look you up and ask you point-blank…" He fixed Eli with a steely gaze. "What are your intentions toward my niece?"

Eli blinked once and set his mug down on the counter. "Exactly what did Frankie tell you?" he asked, curious.

"Nothing you don't already know," Harry growled.

"Humor me," Eli said, his gaze holding Harry's.

"She said the two of you have not only been dating—you've been sleeping together."

"Did she?"

"Yes, she did," Harry said. "In fact, I believe she said it was hot, sweaty and fabulous. Then she said she might be pregnant already, given how often the two of you have been going at it. Which is why I'm asking you—what the hell do you intend to do about Frankie?"

Stunned, Eli stared at Harry for a full minute as he tried to absorb the surprising information. Then a slow smile curved his lips. "Harry, I can guarantee you I don't plan to do anything that would harm Frankie, nor anything she doesn't want me to do."

"That didn't answer my question." Harry's brows lowered.

"No, it didn't." Eli unbuckled his tool belt and slung it on the counter behind him. "And with all due respect for your concern about Frankie, and your long relationship as her adopted uncle, I'm not going to answer it." He shrugged out of his safety vest and hung it on the high back of the drafter's stool.

"Wolf Construction and Dean Construction are the final two companies being considered to build the Hunt-Com campus," Harry said. "Whether or not you plan to marry Frankie could make a big difference as to who's awarded the contract."

Eli stiffened, anger roaring through his veins.

"Harry, I've known you a long time, and I've always had the greatest respect for you." His voice turned colder. "But if you think you can make Frankie a part of some business deal, you're dead wrong. Give the contract to Dean Construction—I don't want it."

He turned on his heel and in two long strides, reached the door.

"Well, I'll be damned." Harry's mellow tones held amazed delight. "You love her."

Eli froze, hand on the door latch. He looked over his shoulder, frowning at Harry. "I never said I love Frankie."

"You don't have to." Harry's grin lit his entire face. "I've known you since you were a kid, and over the years I've watched you build your father and grandfather's company into a powerhouse. There's no way you'd turn down a contract like HuntCom's unless you had a powerful incentive. And that's love," he added, beaming.

Eli shook his head at Harry's insistence. Over the last few days, he'd privately acknowledged to himself that he was in love with Frankie. But he'd be damned if he told Harry before he bared his heart to her. "Believe what you like, Harry, but leave Frankie alone. And don't encourage Nicholas again." His voice was a low, threatening growl.

"Of course I won't," Harry replied with alacrity. "She's obviously taken." He rubbed his hands together, clearly relishing what he thought was a match between Eli and Frankie.

Eli could have groaned aloud. He bit off a hot retort about the older man's interference in Frankie's life. "Think what you like, Harry, but stop looking for men to send after Frankie."

And with that, Eli shoved open the door and left the trailer, loping down the wooden steps to his truck. As he backed out of his parking slot and left the lot, he saw Harry exit the trailer, standing on the wooden steps with the evening breeze lifting his black hair, a satisfied smile on his face as he watched Eli depart.

Eli wanted to drive straight to Frankie's condo and talk to her, but he knew she was having dinner with her mother tonight. Besides, he was muddy after a day spent on the job site, so he reined in his impatience and instead went home, where he showered, shaved and changed clothes before driving to Queen Anne. He made a stop at Ballard Blossom to pick up a bouquet of flowers.

It was barely seven-thirty when he knocked on her door.

"Eli." Frankie opened the door, surprise and pleasure easily readable on her features. "I didn't know you were coming over tonight. I thought you had a meeting."

"I did—but I decided not to go." Eli hadn't given the meeting another thought after Harry told him about Frankie's declaration. He stepped inside, closing the door as he held out the flowers.

"Oh, Eli, they're lovely." Frankie cradled the bouquet, dropping her head to inhale, her lashes lowering. "They smell marvelous—just like spring." Her brown eyes were soft as she looked up at him. "How did you know I was wishing for winter to go away today?"

"I didn't. I just wanted to see you smile, and since you love flowers, I figured these would do it."

Her lush mouth curved, her brown eyes warm as she met his gaze. "You were right," she murmured. She waved her hand toward the living room. "Why don't you have a seat? I'll put these in water."

Eli followed her into the kitchen, leaning against the

doorjamb to watch as she went up on her toes to reach a shelf above the sink.

She wore a pair of dark green knit pants with a tie at the waist. As she stretched to reach a crystal vase on an upper shelf, her short-sleeve white knit top rode up to reveal a strip of soft pale skin and the delicate indentation of her navel above the waistband of the green pants. Her blond hair was loose, brushing against her shoulders as she turned her head to look at him.

"Have you had dinner?" she asked, casting a sideways glance at him before running tap water into the vase.

"I grabbed a sandwich at home." He didn't tell her he'd eaten it in three bites while he stripped off muddy clothes before showering.

"If you're still hungry, Mom sent beef Stroganoff and pineapple cheesecake home with me."

Eli was tempted. But other things were uppermost in his mind, so he shook his head. "Thanks, but I'm good."

Finished with arranging the fragrant blue, pink and white blooms, Frankie picked up the vase and walked past him into the living room. Eli followed her, tensing as she bent to set the vase on the coffee table, the soft green knit pulling tight over the curve of her bottom as she did so.

"I'm glad you're here, Eli, I have something I wanted to talk to you about and didn't want to do it over the phone." She turned and found Eli so close that she effectively stepped into his arms. "Oh." Startled, she clutched his biceps.

He settled his hands at her waist, steadying her.

"I had a visit from Harry today," he told her, watching intently for her reaction.

Frankie groaned and closed her eyes, then opened them to look up at him. "I'm afraid to ask why," she said.

"He wanted to know my intentions."

"Your intentions? About what?" She frowned at him, puzzled.

"You," Eli said succinctly.

She stared at him, still clearly puzzled, before understanding dawned. She flushed, color moving up her throat to stain her cheeks a deeper pink. "I'm going to kill him," she muttered. "I suppose he told you about my conversation with him and Mom last night?"

"Part of it," Eli confirmed.

"I was afraid of that," she told him. "That's what I wanted to talk to you about tonight, Eli. I'm afraid I lost my temper with Harry and told him we're sleeping together."

"That's what he said." Eli tugged her forward until her thighs rested against his. "He also said you thought it was hot, sweaty and fabulous."

Frankie's face turned pinker, but her brown gaze remained on his. "Yes, that's what I said. But, Eli, I lost my temper," she repeated. "Not that it's an excuse for lying," she added hastily. "Harry had just finished telling Mom I was likely to have more university degrees by the time I was forty but not children." Her eyes sparked with anger. "He all but said I was too much of a bookish nerd to attract a man."

"Harry's an idiot." Eli was dumbfounded. "Where did he get the idea you couldn't get a man? You're beautiful and sexy as hell. You must have men following you around with their tongues hanging out."

Startled, Frankie laughed with delight. She slipped her arms around his neck. "You're such a charmer, Eli."

"No, I'm just stating the obvious." He urged her closer. "I'm glad you told Harry and your mom we're sleeping together. Because it gave me hope. I don't think you would have said that in front of your mother if you weren't ready for it to be true."

Her eyes widened. "I'm not sure I—"

Eli bent his head and stopped her protests by covering her mouth with his. The soft curves of her body already rested trustingly against the harder angles of his, and she murmured with pleasure when he stroked one hand up her spine to cup the back of her head. Her hair was pale silk against his fingers, her soft curves willing as he urged her closer.

"Honey," he said, reluctantly releasing her mouth to lift his head and look down at her. Only inches separated them. Her thick-lashed brown eyes were dazed, eyelids heavy, and her soft mouth was faintly swollen from the pressure of his. "Take me to bed." He stroked his tongue over the lush fullness of her lower lip, tasting her, and she shuddered.

"Yes," she murmured against his lips.

She slipped her hands from his neck, catching his hand to tug him with her into her bedroom. She stopped next to her bed and began unbuttoning his shirt, slipping the buttons through the holes with slow concentration. She tugged the shirttails out of his jeans and pushed the white cotton off his shoulders.

Eli grabbed the white T-shirt he wore underneath and yanked it up and off over his head, tossing it behind him on the floor. Frankie murmured, a soft hum of approval. He shuddered when she flattened her palms on his abdomen, tracing the swell of muscles.

The fascination on her face was arousing as hell. Eli stood it as long as he could, loving the feel of her hands on him, before he bent and took her mouth with his in a quick, hard kiss. He slipped his hands under the hem of her cotton T-shirt and pulled it up, her hair drawn upward to expose the arch of her throat and nape, then tumbling to her shoulders when he tugged the shirt off over her head. Beneath it, she wore a pale green lace and satin bra. Pretty though it was, Eli wanted her naked.

He wrapped his arms around her and a moment later, tugged the bra free and slid the straps down her arms. He froze, hands on her waist, and stared.

Frankie was awash in pleasure. It took her a moment to realize Eli had gone still. She swept her tumbled hair behind one ear and looked up to find his eyes heavy-lidded and intent, smoky with arousal.

"You're so beautiful," he muttered, his voice rasping, deeper than a moment before.

His hands stroked upward from her waist, tracing

over her rib cage. He eased her closer, his thumbs brushing the lower curve of her breasts. Then one arm swept around her waist, bending her backward as his mouth took hers and one hand cupped her breast. Frankie shuddered when his thumb stroked over the sensitive, taut nipple, and she strained closer, pushing against him, wanting more contact.

Eli groaned, his lips tasting the underside of her chin, the curve of her throat and upper swell of her breast before his mouth closed over the tip. Frankie twisted against him, shivering with pleasure, her arms holding him closer. The heat between them rose higher.

Impatient, Eli shoved the knit pants down her legs and hooked his thumbs under the lace-covered bikini panties over her hips. He eased them down her legs and off before tumbling her backward onto the bed. She held out her arms, waiting as he shoved his jeans and boxers off before joining her.

The hard angles of his body settled against hers, and Frankie welcomed his solid weight. Her breasts were crushed softly against the powerful muscles of his chest; Frankie twisted, loving the slide of his skin against the sensitive tips.

Eli took her mouth, nudging her knees apart with his thigh. Frankie shuddered, wanting him even closer, and wrapped her legs around his waist. Groaning, he flexed his hips and with a powerful surge, joined them. She cried out, arching beneath him, and the world narrowed to the man above her, heat raging out of control until they both shuddered, falling over the edge together.

* * *

"Good morning, sunshine."

Frankie muttered and burrowed deeper into her pillow.

"Time to wake up."

She could swear her dream had somehow added aromas to its visual and audio dimensions. She frowned, half awake.

Eli's lips brushed over her temple. "Honey, are you always like this in the morning?" His deep voice held amusement, layered with affection.

Frankie opened one eye. Eli was sprawled across his side of the bed, his head propped on one hand. The smile on his face was sinfully sexy—and he held a mug of steaming coffee a few inches from her nose.

"You brought me coffee?"

"It's yours if you'll sit up," he told her, his smile widening.

Sighing, Frankie levered upright, clutching the sheet to her chest, and shoved her pillow behind her against the headboard.

"I'm up." She yawned, covering her mouth with one hand, and considered him through half-open eyes.

He caught her hand, curled her fingers around the mug and grinned at her. "You're cute when you're comatose."

"You brought me coffee. Therefore, I'll let you get away with that." She yawned again, settling back against the pillow and smiling sleepily. "I could get used to this," she told him.

"Uh-huh." He bunched up his pillow against the headboard and stretched out beside her, his big frame taking up more than his share of the bed. He leaned sideways, gathered her up and shifted her closer, bracing her back against his chest, his arms wrapped around her waist.

"Hey," she protested. "You could have spilled my coffee."

"But I didn't." He nuzzled the back of her neck, moving her hair aside until his lips found the sensitive skin of her neck.

Frankie closed her eyes, smiling contentedly. "This is a very nice way to wake up." Her voice was throaty, bemused.

"Yeah, isn't it?" His lips trailed down the curve of her throat to her shoulder, and she tipped her head to give him better access. He tugged the sheet lower, his hands replacing the soft cotton as he cupped her breasts. "I like it. A lot."

The alarm on the bedside table went off, and the radio came on, the voice of the morning announcer bright and cheery.

"Darn." Frankie stirred, lifting her head. "I have a breakfast meeting this morning," she said regretfully.

"Skip it." Eli brushed a kiss against the soft, vulnerable skin just beneath her ear.

Frankie closed her eyes as the world began to slowly spin. "I can't," she got out. "I have to give a report."

"Damn." Reluctantly, Eli released her.

She turned her head, her lips meeting his. The kiss

was sweet and long, and Frankie was reluctant to end it. But at last she sat up to deposit her mug on the bedside table before slipping out of bed.

"Want some help showering?" Eli asked as she entered the bathroom.

A quick glance over her shoulder told her he'd watched her walk naked out of the room. She flushed. "No, thanks. If you help, I'll take twice as long, and I'll miss my meeting."

"Yeah, but you'll have twice as much fun."

"Sorry, but no." She laughed at his disappointed expression and closed the bathroom door.

They left her apartment together, Eli opening Frankie's car door and kissing her breathless before he walked away. His truck was parked on the street, and as she left the condo's parking garage, she waved. He lifted a hand in reply, his handsome face creasing in a smile as he watched her drive away.

Frankie realized she was smiling, happiness bubbling up from inside. She was in love. She wanted to tell the world.

So why hadn't she told Eli?

A better question was: If he felt the same, why hadn't he told her?

Last night had been wonderful. Making love with Eli was everything she'd hoped and dreamed it would be. She no longer had any doubts about her feelings for him, but she was uncharacteristically reluctant to tell him how she felt. Not until she had some indication he felt the same.

She didn't like being unsure of herself.

This is one of the reasons I never wanted to fall in love, she thought with a sigh. *I'm uncomfortably vulnerable and unsure of him. Why didn't I just ask him?*

She knew why—but she hated to admit it, even to herself.

Because she knew, she would have been devastated if Eli had told her he didn't love her in return.

Chapter Fourteen

Frankie set aside her worries over Eli's long-term intentions, instead focusing on the amazing night she'd spent in his arms. Happiness bubbled through her veins, and she had the urge to call Tommi and Bobbie to tell them she totally understood why they seemed to glow. Falling in love did that for a woman, she thought.

She had only two morning classes. When she left the lecture hall and hurried back to her office, she was still walking on air. Planning to visit Lily's boutique and buy new lingerie, she grabbed her purse and raincoat and left the hall to hurry to her car. She'd just tossed her purse onto the passenger seat and switched on the engine when her cell phone rang.

"Hello?" Her brain was fully occupied with wondering whether Eli liked black lingerie or if he preferred

red. Distracted, she didn't catch the first words the caller spoke. "I'm sorry, who is this?" she asked, holding the phone to her ear with her left hand while her right fitted the key into the ignition.

"This is Matt, Eli's brother."

"Hi, Matt." Wondering why Eli's brother would be calling her, Frankie switched on the engine.

"Connor thought I should call and let you know there's been an accident. Eli's fine, but we thought he might want you to know."

Frankie froze, her heart seeming to stop beating.

"Where is he?"

"He's in the ER at Harborview."

"Harborview?" Frankie's veins turned to ice. She knew serious trauma cases were taken directly to Harborview. "How badly is he hurt?"

"The doc isn't sure. They're still running tests."

"What happened?" Her fingers gripped the steering wheel, knuckles whitening.

"That damned slope above the job site slid on the east side." Matt's voice was taut with anger and disgust. "Took out a big fir just past the work trailer and caught Eli's truck. He was running to move it out of the way when one of the big tree limbs caught him."

"Oh, my God." Frankie caught her breath.

"The doc's running an MRI now. I'll call you back when we hear the results, okay?"

"Yes," Frankie managed to get out. "Okay."

She dropped her phone into her purse and waited a moment, willing her fingers to stop trembling. Then she left the parking lot, heading across town to the hospital.

The parking at Harborview was nonexistent. Frankie drove through the stacked levels of the huge garage twice before finally finding a spot. She breathed a sigh of relief and quickly nosed her car into the open space before hurrying toward the elevator, her heels tapping quickly on the cement as she ran.

When she left the elevator, it took her fifteen minutes to find her way through the maze of hallways. Harborview was Seattle's general hospital, and not only were serious trauma and accident patients seen there, but also those folks without insurance. Consequently, the halls were thronged with a variety of people, from the homeless to well-dressed businessmen to middle-income housewives.

At last, Frankie reached the emergency area and found the waiting room. But none of Eli's brothers were there—she didn't recognize any of the people seated in the chairs or ranged on the two sofas.

Terrified, she left the waiting room and stopped a nurse in green scrubs just outside.

"I'm looking for an accident patient. He's supposed to be in the ER—his name is Eli Wolf."

The nurse eyed her shrewdly. "Are you a family member?"

"He's my fiancé." Frankie lied without a shred of regret.

"Then I'm sure it's okay for you to go in. This way." The nurse held open the heavy door and led Frankie into a big room sectioned off with curtains that slid on overhead transoms. Several of the curtains were open, the beds within their semicircles empty.

The nurse led her across the room. Just as she pulled back a section of the heavy drape, masculine laughter rang out.

"He's in here," the nurse told her, standing back to let Frankie pass.

Frankie stepped quickly through the opening and stopped abruptly, her eyes filling with tears.

Eli was propped up in the raised hospital bed, his chest bare above the white sheet bunched at his waist. Red scrapes marred the left side of his chest, and bruises left faint blue marks. But he'd been laughing, a smile still curving his mouth and lighting his eyes.

Ethan and Connor sat in plastic chairs, long legs stretched out, while Matt stood at the foot of the bed.

They all looked up when she stepped into the room.

Frankie's frantic gaze tracked over what she could see of Eli's body. She was relieved to find nothing worse than scrapes and bruises. The tight knot squeezing her chest and sitting like lead just below her collarbone eased, but the tears streaming down her face didn't stop.

She brushed at them with trembling fingertips while she stared at Eli, unable to speak.

"Frankie," his deep voice rumbled. "Honey, I'm all right."

She didn't speak, and the tears wouldn't stop falling.

Her feet wouldn't move; they felt cemented to the floor.

"I'll see you guys later," Eli said without taking his eyes from Frankie. "Thanks for coming down."

"Yeah, no problem." Metal chair legs scraped against the linoleum-covered floor as Ethan and Connor stood. Matt joined them, and the three filed out, each pausing to awkwardly pat Frankie's shoulder as they passed.

"Come here, honey." Eli opened his arms. The words lifted the paralysis that held her. At last, Frankie could move.

She ran across the waxed floor. Eli caught her hand and tugged her down onto the hospital bed, facing him. And when he wrapped his arms around her, she willingly let him tuck her close, her face pressed against the strong column of his throat, his pulse beating with rhythmic thuds against her cheek.

"You scared me." She ran her hands over him, searching for breaks. Remembering the scrapes on his side, she carefully backed away from him, although he didn't let her go far. The raw places on his ribs looked like rug burns, and she winced as she barely skimmed her fingertips over one. "This looks sore."

He shrugged, the hard muscles of his chest shifting under her hand. "They're just a few little scrapes."

"What caused them?"

"I don't remember exactly, but I think it was the branches of the fir tree." He shook his head in disgust. "I knew that slope was going to slide sooner or later. We're just lucky it only gave way on one end."

"Did you have to be standing there when it did?" she demanded, smoothing her fingertips over the bruise on his cheekbone before cupping his cheek.

"I didn't exactly plan it that way," he told her, a small, endearing smile lifting the corners of his mouth. "If I'd had a choice, trust me, I would have been on the other side of the lot with Connor."

"Humph." Frankie wasn't mollified. She continued to stroke her fingers over the warm, satiny skin of his chest, the feel of his hard muscles and the lift of his chest as he breathed soothing the terror that had shaken her. Suddenly, she stiffened and sat up. "Eli, you're bruised on your left side. Did the tree damage your left leg—the one you broke last year?"

"No." He pulled her back, tucking her head beneath his chin. "That's why the doctor scheduled me for an MRI. Well, that and the general beating I got all over from the tree," he conceded. "But the leg is fine. I'm sure I'll be stiff and sore tomorrow, and probably for a few days to come, but ultimately I was incredibly lucky. No serious damage."

"Thank goodness." Frankie hugged him tighter before instantly loosening her grip. "Sorry, I didn't mean to hurt you."

His arms pressed her close once again. "You didn't hurt me." He brushed a kiss against her hair. "The accident was a wake-up call for me, Frankie. I could have died this afternoon without telling you how much I love you. I should have told you last night—or this morning. I don't know why I didn't. Yes, I do," he said with a shake of his head. "I chickened out because I was afraid you weren't ready to hear it." His arms tightened, pressing her closer, and his voice rumbled. "I couldn't stop thinking about you after we kissed at your birthday party. If you hadn't walked into the office and asked me to help you, I would have called and asked you out. I wasn't just pretending to be interested in you—I wanted to spend time with you and this was the perfect opportunity." He paused, his voice deeper when he continued. "We hadn't been dating for more than a week when I knew I was in deep trouble. You weren't just another beautiful woman. I didn't want to admit it, even to myself, but I'd fallen in love with you."

"Eli," she breathed, tilting her head back to look up at him. "I love you, too. I wanted to tell you last night, but I wasn't sure you felt the same way about me."

His eyes flared, hot with blue fire, and he bent his head and kissed her. The warm pressure of his mouth reaffirmed he was safe, his injuries minor, and her earlier terror that she'd lost him melted away.

When he lifted his head, his blue eyes were heavy-lidded and darkened. "Harry asked me yesterday what my intentions were toward you, Frankie. I want to spend my life with you. I want to wake up in the morning with you in my arms and go to bed at night with you beside me. I want you to marry me. I want us to have a little girl who looks just like you and makes me sit on little chairs to play at tea parties." He stroked his thumb over the faintly swollen fullness of her lower lip. "But most of all, I want you to love me the way I love you. I wasn't sure that was possible, but when you walked in here, I began to hope."

"Oh, Eli." Frankie's eyes filled, and tears spilled down her cheeks. "I love you so much it scares me."

"Scares you?" He frowned. "Why?"

"Because loving someone this much is a scary thing for me. I was very young when my father died, but I remember watching my mother grieve and thinking I never wanted to love someone that much, and I've never let myself fall in love. Until now—I can't control how I feel about you. It's as if you're the other half of me, as if I didn't even realize I needed you until we started dating." She shook her head. "Like I said, loving you is scary. I've never done it before. I'm in uncharted territory."

He smiled slowly. "If it helps, honey, you're not alone."

"Really?" She searched his face. "You've never been in love like this before, either?"

"No."

"Good," she said firmly. "Then we can muddle through together."

"I'm game for anything we can do together, honey," he said. "How soon do you think we can spring me from this place?"

"I don't know. Certainly not until the doctor has run all the tests he needs to be sure you're all right."

"I'm fine. And I'll be better as soon as we're home." He lifted a questioning brow. "My place or yours? I don't care which, just pick one. But you're spending tonight with me."

"Only if the doctor says it's okay," she warned him.

"Honey, I'm not asking the doc if I can make love to you tonight," he told her with a slow grin. "It wouldn't matter if he told me yes or no. But if you'll go find him, we can get me released and out of this place. Unless you want to climb under the sheet with me and get creative?"

Frankie laughed and slipped off the bed. "You're incorrigible. I'll see if I can find a nurse."

Once again, family and friends gathered at Harry's lakeside mansion. This time to celebrate Eli's release from the hospital and his engagement to Frankie.

The panel of doors between the living room and an adjacent family room were thrown open, and the space was crowded with guests. Harry had spared no expense—tables groaning under the weight of catered food and champagne fountains flowing.

At the end of the room, standing near the ebony grand piano with the Seattle skyline visible through the floor-to-ceiling windows behind them, Harry and Cornelia stood apart, savoring a moment alone.

"Well, Harry—" Cornelia lifted her champagne glass, sipping as she eyed his tall, lanky figure and the smile wreathing his features "—all has turned out well. I've never seen Frankie so happy. She absolutely glows."

"And Eli looks pretty happy, too," Harry agreed. He lifted his glass, touching it to Cornelia's with a small click of congratulations. "Here's to another wedding in the family."

"I'll drink to that." Cornelia sipped once more, sighing contentedly as she looked about the room. "It was lovely of you to volunteer to hold Frankie's engagement party here, Harry. We could have had it at my house, but I'm not sure we would have all fit."

"It's my pleasure." Harry's eyes gleamed, his gaze intent on Cornelia as she smiled and waved at Tommi, standing with Max, Bobbie and Gabriel across the room.

Their moment of quiet conversation was all too short, and soon Cornelia was called away by a group of Frankie's high school friends. Harry let her go and moved through the crowd, visiting with friends and greeting some guests he hadn't met before. One of those was Eli's grandfather, Jack, who accepted with alacrity Harry's offer of whisky instead of champagne.

"Nice of you to throw this party for Eli," Jack told Harry.

The two older men stood at the end of the long living room, heavy lead crystal glasses containing a few inches of whisky in their hands.

"Glad to do it," Harry said expansively. "He's been practically a member of the family for years." He nodded at the newly engaged couple holding court near the fireplace halfway down the room. "And now that he's engaged to my niece, he'll be making it official. Seems like a natural next step."

"Does that mean Wolf Construction gets the contract

to build HuntCom's new campus?" Jack asked casually, his blue eyes shrewd as he looked at Harry.

"Of course." Harry's eyes twinkled. "Can't have my niece's fiancé out of work."

Jack chuckled. "Good to know my grandson is marrying into a family that understands taking care of its own."

"There will be other opportunities, too, of course," Harry told him. "HuntCom has facilities outside Seattle, some overseas."

"I'd just as soon the boys worked closer to home, especially now that Eli's going to be married," Jack told him. "It's hard to keep a wife happy and be a good dad from half a world away."

"True." Harry nodded his agreement.

Jack's deep laugh was clearly audible over the murmur of conversation. Frankie looked at Eli's grandfather, finding him in deep conversation with Harry, and felt a niggle of foreboding. Arm hooked through Eli's, she leaned against his side and went up on tiptoe to reach him. He bent his head.

"Eli, your grandfather and Harry look like they're plotting," she whispered in his ear. "Should we be worried?"

He glanced up and across the room, covering her hand with his where it rested on his sleeve. "No," he reassured her. "Harry's a cagey guy, but Granddad can run him a close second. They're probably telling each other stories about the business deals they've wangled, trying to top each other."

"You know," Frankie said slowly, watching the two older men and the ease they seemed to feel with each other. "I'm wondering if we made a mistake getting those two together. Jack Wolf might be the only man I ever met who can match Harry's willingness to tell his family members what to do."

Eli laughed and bent to brush a kiss against her cheek. "How did you figure that out about Granddad so quickly?"

"I've had a couple of conversations with him over the last few days," she told him. "And he doesn't pull his punches. He wants us to have a baby—soon."

"He told you that?" Eli demanded, a frown growing.

"Yes, but don't be angry with him." Frankie smoothed her fingertip over the frown lines, easing them away. "I told him Harry had already informed me that I'm soon going to be past my best childbearing years and I'd duly noted the information."

"Damn, Frankie." Eli's voice held admiration. "I think Granddad finally met his match in you."

Her mouth curved in a small smile. "That's what he said."

Eli hugged her, laughter rumbling as he did.

"Are you sure we shouldn't warn Georgie about Harry?" Frankie said, still concerned. "It's not like Harry to abandon a project, and he seems obsessed with matchmaking."

"No, I don't think so. After all," Eli said, "look how well his meddling worked out for us."

"But we got together while trying to avoid Harry's scheming," she reminded him.

"But the end result was the same. Harry meddled in your love life, and, in the end, you and I are together." Eli tipped up her chin, his eyes a deep, smoky blue behind half-lowered lashes.

"That's true," Frankie agreed. "And how amazingly wonderful is that?"

"Pretty damned incredible," Eli said fervently. He bent his head, his mouth covering hers.

Yes, she thought as the kiss swept her under. She adored him more than she'd ever thought possible, more than her long-ago crush. And even more astounding, he loved her, too.

Life stretched before her, filled with infinite happy possibilities. Frankie wrapped her arms around his neck and kissed him back, unaware that the roomful of guests was cheering with delight.

* * * * *

Silhouette®

COMING NEXT MONTH

Available January 25, 2011

SPECIAL EDITION

#2095 DONOVAN'S CHILD
Christine Rimmer
Bravo Family Ties

#2096 HEALING DR. FORTUNE
Judy Duarte
The Fortunes of Texas: Lost...and Found

#2097 CINDY'S DOCTOR CHARMING
Teresa Southwick
Men of Mercy Medical

#2098 HIS DAUGHTER...THEIR CHILD
Karen Rose Smith
Reunion Brides

#2099 MEET MR. PRINCE
Patricia Kay
The Hunt for Cinderella

#2100 THE PRINCE'S SECOND CHANCE
Brenda Harlen
Reigning Men

REQUEST YOUR FREE BOOKS!
2 FREE NOVELS PLUS 2 FREE GIFTS!

SPECIAL EDITION
Life, Love and Family!

YES! Please send me 2 FREE Silhouette® Special Edition® novels and my 2 FREE gifts (gifts are worth about $10). After receiving them, if I don't wish to receive any more books, I can return the shipping statement marked "cancel." If I don't cancel, I will receive 6 brand-new novels every month and be billed just $4.24 per book in the U.S. or $4.99 per book in Canada. That's a saving of 15% off the cover price! It's quite a bargain! Shipping and handling is just 50¢ per book.* I understand that accepting the 2 free books and gifts places me under no obligation to buy anything. I can always return a shipment and cancel at any time. Even if I never buy another book from Silhouette, the two free books and gifts are mine to keep forever.

235/335 SDN E5RG

Name _____ (PLEASE PRINT) _____

Address _____ Apt. #

City _____ State/Prov. _____ Zip/Postal Code

Signature (if under 18, a parent or guardian must sign)

Mail to the Silhouette Reader Service:
IN U.S.A.: P.O. Box 1867, Buffalo, NY 14240-1867
IN CANADA: P.O. Box 609, Fort Erie, Ontario L2A 5X3

Not valid for current subscribers to Silhouette Special Edition books.

Want to try two free books from another line?
Call 1-800-873-8635 or visit www.morefreebooks.com.

* Terms and prices subject to change without notice. Prices do not include applicable taxes. N.Y. residents add applicable sales tax. Canadian residents will be charged applicable provincial taxes and GST. Offer not valid in Quebec. This offer is limited to one order per household. All orders subject to approval. Credit or debit balances in a customer's account(s) may be offset by any other outstanding balance owed by or to the customer. Please allow 4 to 6 weeks for delivery. Offer available while quantities last.

Your Privacy: Silhouette is committed to protecting your privacy. Our Privacy Policy is available online at www.eHarlequin.com or upon request from the Reader Service. From time to time we make our lists of customers available to reputable third parties who may have a product or service of interest to you. If you would prefer we not share your name and address, please check here. ☐

Help us get it right—We strive for accurate, respectful and relevant communications. To clarify or modify your communication preferences, visit us at www.ReaderService.com/consumerschoice.

SSE10R

Try these Healthy and Delicious Spring Rolls!

INGREDIENTS

2 packages rice-paper spring roll wrappers (20 wrappers)

1 cup grated carrot

¼ cup bean sprouts

1 cucumber, julienned

1 red bell pepper, without stem and seeds, julienned

4 green onions finely chopped— use only the green part

DIRECTIONS

1. Soak one rice-paper wrapper in a large bowl of hot water until softened.

2. Place a pinch each of carrots, sprouts, cucumber, bell pepper and green onion on the wrapper toward the bottom third of the rice paper.

3. Fold ends in and roll tightly to enclose filling.

4. Repeat with remaining wrappers. Chill before serving.

Find this and many more delectable recipes including the perfect dipping sauce in

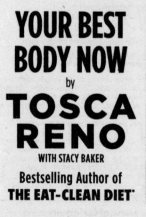

YOUR BEST BODY NOW

by

TOSCA RENO

WITH STACY BAKER

Bestselling Author of
THE EAT-CLEAN DIET®

Available wherever books are sold!

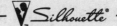

ROMANTIC SUSPENSE

Sparked by Danger, Fueled by Passion.

NEW YORK TIMES BESTSELLING AUTHOR

RACHEL LEE

No Ordinary Hero

Strange noises...a woman's mysterious disappearance
and a killer on the loose who's too close for comfort.

With no where else to turn, Delia Carmody looks
to her aloof neighbour to help, only to discover
that Mike Windwalker is no ordinary hero.

Available in February.
Wherever books are sold.